Books by Barbara Corcoran

Meet Me at Tamerlane's Tomb
A Dance to Still Music
All the Summer Voices
The Winds of Time
Don't Slam the Door When You Go
A Trick of Light
This Is a Recording
The Long Journey
A Row of Tigers
Sasha, My Friend
Sam

MEET ME AT TAMERLANE'S TOMB

MEET ME AT TAMERLANE'S TOMB

Barbara Corcoran

ILLUSTRATED BY CHARLES ROBINSON

ATHENEUM 1975 NEW YORK

Copyright © 1975 By Barbara Corcoran
Published simultaneously in Canada by
McClelland & Stewart, Ltd.
Manufactured in the United States of America by
H. Wolff, New York
Designed by Harriett Barton
First Edition

Library of Congress Cataloging in Publication Data
Corcoran, Barbara.
Meet me at Tamerlane's tomb.

SUMMARY: While on a trip to Samarkand with her
family, a fat, awkward fourteen-year-old discovers her
own strong points during an inadvertent involvement
with drug smugglers.

I. Robinson, Charles, illus. II. Title.
PZ7.C814Me [Fic] 74-19351
ISBN 0-689-30446-3

FOR ANNE AND SAM WITH LOVE AND THANKS

MEET ME AT TAMERLANE'S TOMB

one

MY MOTHER, who is beautiful, languorous and terribly feminine, usually tells people that when I was born, she took one look and said, "Women's lib." My father, who is handsome and not a bit languorous, likes to add, "We haven't decided whether to send her to truck driving school or train her for the Green Bay Packers." And my big sister, Penny, puts in her two cents' worth: "The fat farm," she says, "is where she belongs."

Be that as it may, here I was on a moonlight night,

gazing at the tomb of Tamerlane, in the city of Samarkand, which dates from the fourth millennium B.C., and I wasn't thinking about Tamerlane at all; I was thinking about the fact that I was hopelessly, unrequitedly, nauseatingly, marvelously in love. With my sister's boyfriend.

Back at the hotel he would be playing the drums right now in the not really very good little band that played old American pop songs very loud while the tourists ate late dinner. It was a traveling Czech band, and it was my impression that he was not a Czech, but he never said what he was, and he wasn't the kind of person you would ask. My sister Penny always said he was Swiss, but she was just guessing, and she picked Swiss because it was respectable. His name was Paul, which could have been almost anything. My father said he spoke Russian with what sounded to him like a Slavic accent. My father teaches Russian, in upper New York State, which is why we were spending three weeks in the Soviet Union, which was going to make us two weeks late for school, a fact I did not like because I am on the track team; and we always work out some in the fall before it gets too cold. But our visas were delayed so we had to come when we could. We had already been to Moscow, Leningrad, and Tbilisi, and one night in Tashkent between planes; and now we were spending the last lap in Samarkand.

4

I watched the moon inch up behind the enormous blue dome of the mausoleum, and I thought about Tamerlane and his solid jade coffin, and the coffins of his relatives and his teacher. And then I thought of Paul, with his beautiful sculptured-looking head. He had dark longish hair, which you don't see on Russians, and his eyes were dark, watchful and often full of laughter even when he didn't laugh out loud. But the most remarkable thing was his nose. Kind of an Arabic nose, it was, narrow and a little bit hooked with nostrils that flared sometimes like a thorough-bred horse's. I got the feeling he smelled out situations. Or maybe he just didn't like the smell of burning mutton that was always in the air. Penny objects to my calling it burning mutton. She says shashlik is a delicacy that people come from all over the world to taste. I doubt that very much. And a rose by any other name is burned mutton to me. I didn't like shashlik, and my brother Andrew got very sick from eating some that he bought from a street vendor. Burned mutton was what it was.

An old man in a blue long flowing robe and a white turban went by, driving a little two-wheeled donkey cart. Those donkeys are very sweet. The Intourist guide stopped me from taking a picture of one. She said I shouldn't photograph poor people. It was really the donkey I wanted a picture of, more than the man, and I doubt if the donkey's pride would have been hurt. In the other places we'd been, the people didn't look poor, but in Samarkand they did. It was kind of a dignified poverty, though. Centuries ago it had been one of the greatest and richest cities in the world, and now it wasn't, but you felt the greatness and power still. There was nothing mean or squalid. Those old men had so much pride in their long narrow faces—like wrinkled paper—and their white beards and piercing black eyes. They reminded me of Old Testament prophets, although, of course, they were Mohammedan, not Christian. Intourist needn't have worried, because they were not people anyone could patronize.

A young policeman walked by in the shadows of the big trees. I thought of the man on our plane whom I had nicknamed the Menace. I wondered if he would strike a policeman as menacing, or if it was what my father called my feverish imagination. The man told us he was a Turk. My mother thought he was very pleasant, but that tends to be her reaction to people unless they're downright revolting. The Turk was a tall man in Western-type clothes, who limped. I always expected to see a scar on his face, but there wasn't one. Andrew said maybe he covered it up with makeup. Andrew shared my view of the Turk, only he thought he was the reincarnation of Tamerlane. Andrew is big on reincarnation, and, as he pointed out, Tamerlane also was lame. But I don't believe in reincarnation.

I walked back to the hotel, enjoying the warm evening air and trying to picture how the place had looked when Alexander the Great stopped by, or when Genghis Khan paid a visit. Probably in many ways not so different from the way it looked now, only I suppose a lot busier. Now it seemed like a city dreaming of the past, like an old man who has been terribly great and world-shaking in his younger days, now sitting quietly and remembering.

When I came into the hotel I heard Paul's drums beating out "San Francisco," of all things. I wonder why bands in Russia play old American songs. An Uzbek in a black suit and a black embroidered cap watched me as I went into the lobby. I thought he looked hostile, but my father said that was the way Arab people were apt to look, even if they didn't feel hostile at all. Maybe so. I thought I had seen this man before.

In the dining room I saw my family having dessert. My beautiful mother, my handsome father, my ravishing sister, my cute brother. It seemed a shame to join them and let the world know that such a family had an ugly duckling. But I wanted to sit and watch Paul. I walked across the long room toward them.

When I sidled past the bandstand, I couldn't help taking a quick look at Paul. He blinked his eyes at me without missing a beat or changing expression, and I was happy because that meant hello. When I got to my family's table, I sat down too quickly and almost crushed my father's foot, when he tried to help me with my chair.

Penny looked at the ceiling. ". . . and the lighter-than-air ship came to earth without a tremor . . ."

Because of Paul I was too flustered to answer back.

"Well, there you are," my mother said. "We were worrying about you."

"I was only over at the mausoleum," I said.

My father tied his shoelace, which had somehow come untied in the process of getting me seated. "The mausoleum," he said, "will never replace the corner drugstore." He says things like that, and it

never seems to bother him that he's the only one who thinks they're funny.

The waiters were sitting at a table out in the atrium eating their dinner. Whenever you wanted a waiter at that hotel, you'd find him eating. One of them looked around, and my father beckoned. After a while the man came over and handed me the menu. I knew from experience that anything I wanted would be gone. It was an enormous menu, but only the six or seven things marked with a price were available ever; the rest was just to impress people, I guess.

"Borsch?" I said. The band was playing an oldie-but-goodie called "Stardust," which my father claims he first danced with my mother to.

"Sorry," the waiter said.

"Honey," my father said to my mother, "do you remember the Harvard Jubilee, when I first asked you to dance . . ."

"We all remember it, Dad," my sister said. She was smiling revoltingly at Paul. It was her winsome smile. One of the worst types.

"Pilaf?" I said.

The waiter shook his head. "Shashlik?"

My brother Andrew muttered "excuse me" and got to his feet looking pale. My mother put up her hand, but he left the dining room very rapidly.

My father was humming "Stardust" ". . . a lonely night, dreaming of a song, *da dum di da, dum di da de dum . . .*"

"Andrew is ill again," my mother said. "Oh, dear. I told him not to drink the water."

"It was that rotten mutton," I said. I looked up at the waiter. "I'll just have some fruit and cheese, please."

He gave me his black-eyed look and went away. I wondered if I'd hurt his regional pride about the mutton, but it was unlikely he understood what I said.

"They don't write songs like that anymore," my

father said. "That was Cole Porter at his best."

"Hoagy Carmichael, dear," my mother said.

"Really? I could have sworn it was Porter."

"Doesn't Paul drum divinely," my sister purred.

"Is it possible to drum profanely?" I said. My father laughed.

"I must go look after Andrew," my mother said.

I grabbed her wrist. "Mother, for heaven's sake. Nobody wants to be looked after, when he's in that condition. Let him alone."

"Then I think we should ask for a doctor."

"There's nothing to do, Mother, except not eat." I'd been through it in Moscow; I knew.

"But my poor baby . . ." Mother stopped herself, and smiled a little sheepishly because Penny and I had read her the riot act not long before, about referring to Andrew as her baby. The child is ten years old, after all. I've heard it said that some women feel their life is over when their last child grows up, so I try to be tolerant, but that "my baby" stuff could scar poor old Andy for life.

The band stopped for a break, and my heart began to pound. Penny was suddenly looking away and pretending not to notice Paul. I was scared he would come over and scared he wouldn't. I felt my face getting red. One of my more hideous afflictions is that I blush.

My mother reached over and put the back of her

hand against my cheek. I clenched my teeth. "Mother, please!"

"You look flushed," she said. "Do you feel sick?"

I jerked away. "I feel fine."

"Why is it my children are so delicate?" my father said. "I have enjoyed perfect health all my life."

"Well, don't look at me," my mother said, rather snappishly for her. Illness in her children unnerves her, even when it's entirely imaginary.

"Then who in blazes should I look at?" my father said. "There are only two sets of genes involved here . . ."

And then Penny whirled around, looking surprised, and said, "Why, Paul! How nice." As if she hadn't been making googly eyes at him for hours. "Join us."

"Thank you," he said, in that precise, accented English, in his soul-shaking deep voice. "If I'm not interrupting . . . Good evening, Mrs. Harlow, Mr. Harlow, sir . . ."

"Sit down, Paul, sit down," my father said. "We were just discussing genes."

Hastily, Penny interrupted. "The band was very good tonight."

He made a face. "Sometimes we are bad, sometimes passable; never good."

While Penny and my mother protested, I suffered. He had not said good evening to me. He had ignored me. I know boyfriends aren't very keen on kid sisters, but how could he not know what I felt for him? How could he not feel the vibrations that were rocking me? I pushed back my chair, ready to leave; no one would notice; but then the waiter materialized, putting down, in front of me, an enormous plate of watermelon and three bananas. Nobody could overlook me now.

Paul said. "All for you, Hardy? That looks good."

It wasn't the ideal way to get attention, but beggars can't be choosers. "Want a banana?" I said.

He took one and smiled at me. My insides felt like a toasted marshmallow.

"Not for nothing do we call her Hardy," my sister said. She gave me her sickening big-sister smile. My name is Mary Harding Harlow and I have always been called Hardy to distinguish me from my mother of the same name, but it has always seemed to me that there were other ways of telling us apart.

I positioned a watermelon seed between my teeth and remembered, with nostalgia, the days when I was young enough to spit seeds at my sister. Instead, I had to content myself with smiling my most false smile and staring fixedly at her left eye. This tactic always made her very nervous because she was afraid her eye makeup had smeared. I kept staring until she was very fidgety.

"Who wrote 'Stardust'?" my father said to Paul.

"Hoagy Carmichael, sir."

My mother gave my father a small, smug smile.

"That song really takes me back," my father said, ignoring her.

Paul listened politely while my father told him about the Harvard Jubilee. I could see Penny seething under her smile. She kept giving Mother indignant looks, but Mother was listening and getting all aglow herself this time. You never can tell about grownups.

Paul folded up the banana skin very neatly and placed it on a dish. At that moment it seemed to me that one of the most desirable qualities in a man was neatness. He stood up. "Thank you, Hardy. Now I can perhaps survive the evening." He smiled at me. His teeth were very white and even. And surely that was the most beautiful nose in the whole world.

"You're welcome," I said. Next to my beauty I am noted for my ready wit.

He bowed to my parents. "Thank you. *Auf wiedersehen.*"

When he was out of earshot my mother said, "He must be German."

"Swiss," Penny said.

"Slavic," said my father.

My father finished his glass of hot tea. Train tea, Andrew calls it, because we first had it that way, hot and strong and in a glass, on the train right after the ordeal of going through customs at the border. It was the first time either of us had ever liked tea.

My father heaped up his napkin on the table. "And so to bed."

"Here comes Mr. Kemel," my mother said.

"Oh, bother," my father said.

My sister looked up as Mr. Kemel, the Turkish Menace, approached our table. She fluttered her eyelashes. She thought Mr. Kemel was quote interesting unquote. Which shows you how stupid a man-crazy teen-ager can get. He was old enough to be her father, for heaven's sake.

"Good evening," Mr. Kemel said in his impeccable British accent. "How pleasant to see my American friends again."

"Do join us," my mother said. "We were about to have a second cup of coffee." I am always shocked by the social lies my otherwise honest mother tells.

Mr. Kemel sat down beside Penny and gave her his big inscrutable smile. "And are you enjoying yourself, Miss Penny?"

Penny's eyelashes fluttered like a maddened butterfly. "Yes, really very much. We had a lovely day at the Shah-i Zindar complex. It was fascinating."

Actually Penny had complained bitterly about having to climb all over Shah-i Zindar, though in my opinion it was much the best thing we'd seen. You climbed up to a high, very narrow alley, called the

Street of Dead Town, and off that little street on both sides were all these fabulous tombs and things, really quite big rooms, with all that beautiful mosaic stuff in blue, purple and green, but mostly blue, very intricate designs. It reminded me of a dead version of the Casbah, though to tell you the truth I've never seen the Casbah except in movies.

My father and Mr. Kemel were discussing the exploits of Tamerlane.

"He was a local boy, you know," my father said. "Born a few miles from here. Grew up a regular highway robber."

Mr. Kemel smiled, his mouth making a small crescent under a nose that curved out like a scimitar. "Most of the heroes of history were highway robbers, I suppose, one way or another."

"What an interesting idea," my idiot sister said. Mr. Kemel smiled at her inscrutably.

I wished Andrew were there so we could exchange significant looks when Mr. Kemel mentioned Tamerlane. I studied him secretly while he waved for a waiter (and got one instantly, which my father could never do). He ordered in Russian, and right away there was coffee for everyone and brandy for everyone but me. I wondered what Penny would do with hers. Not that she is averse to a drink, but my father thinks you shouldn't drink until you are pushing forty, or in other words, as old as he is. He reached out and took Penny's glass.

"Too young," he said to Mr. Kemel.

Penny looked furious. Later she would say, "You didn't have to make a scene about it."

I saw Mr. Kemel nod approvingly. Women in this part of the world didn't seem to drink hard liquor. I wondered if he was a Mohammedan. I figured he would be if he thought it was an advantage. He looked sly, I thought, like an old fruit store man I knew at home who always tried to sell you the over-ripe bananas or the sour apples. I thought Andrew was wrong about Mr. Kemel being Tamerlane, even if I had believed in reincarnation. He wasn't tough enough or big enough to be Tamerlane. I wondered what he was really doing in Samarkand. Probably selling the Soviets some slightly moldy Turkish tobacco.

He and my father were talking about safe subjects like space travel and the oil problem and what it was like to live in a small university town in New York State. He seemed quite interested in where we lived and what we did. Paul's band was playing loud music and Mr. Kemel gave them several annoyed looks.

I settled down to Paul-watching. I loved the way he held his head on one side and bent over the drums. I thought he was too good for that second-rate band. I wondered again where he was from and if he had to go with the band whether he wanted to or not. I wasn't too clear about how much choice people had. Had the man who swept the streets dreamed ever since he was a little boy of cleaning streets? Or was he just told to be a streetcleaner? An Intourist woman told us the people worked a forty-hour week, but the floor clerks in this hotel were there all the time, as far as I could see. The woman on our floor slept on a cot beside her desk at night; I'd heard her padding along the corridor in her slippers and knocking on the doors of tourists who were leaving on an early flight. Once I'd opened the door to see if it was really she. And in Tashkent, when we came downstairs before dawn, all the benches in the lobby and the Intourist office were occupied by people asleep. I recognized one of them as a porter, and my father said he thought they were all hotel staff, the cleaning women and so on. I sat down on one man by mistake. He was very nice about it.

As I sat there thinking about this, I was telling it to Paul in my mind. I'd gotten into the habit of talking to him in my mind all the time. Most of it I would never really say to him even if I had the chance. At least not until we'd been married a few years and gotten really acquainted. Just as I thought the word "married," he looked up at the end of a number and smiled at me. I nearly fell off my chair. I am a firm believer in thought transference between sensitive people and I was scared to death that he had read my mind. I began to think very hard about Johnny Whipple back home, so if Paul had gotten my thoughts, he would think he'd made a mistake about who I was thinking of in connection with the word *married*.

I decided it would be safer if I gave my attention to the conversation at the table. Penny was burbling on to Mr. Kemel about how she felt she had been an Oriental woman in some previous incarnation. I happen to know that she doesn't believe in reincarnation; she makes fun of Andrew for believing in it. She was just trying to lead Mr. Kemel down the garden path. I hate to say this about my sister, who is in some ways really okay, but she is an incurable flirt. Right that minute she'd probably forgotten that Paul even existed. And there he was, eating his heart out for her. The trouble with love is everybody falls for the wrong person. Somebody ought to find a way to straighten this out.

My mother was excusing herself on the grounds that she had to look after Andrew, and my father got up with her. I was just dissecting my last chunk of watermelon.

"Come up when you've finished, dear," my mother said.

Mr. Kemel, very suave, said, "Perhaps your lovely daughters would join me in a walk before the evening ends."

I thought of the wide streets, the sidewalks and the strip of park down the middle all shaded and mysterious-looking because of the big poplar trees. It wasn't a place I wanted to stroll in with the Turkish Menace, who was probably a dirty old man at heart. I muttered something about having to write some letters: that's what they always say in English mystery stories when they want to get out of something. So that left Penny. I could see she was thinking it would be romantic to stroll in the moonlight with Mr. Kemel. Suddenly I felt scared. I was afraid something would happen to Penny. I looked at Paul. The music stopped, and he was looking at Penny and Mr. Kemel and he looked upset. I raised my voice so he could hear me.

"Penny, don't forget you promised to have tea with Paul when the band stops playing." I had made it up, and I was afraid she wouldn't go along with it. She frowned and was about to say something, but Paul came quickly to our table. He nodded in a very cold way to Mr. Kemel, which surprised me because I didn't know he knew him.

"We are breaking early," he said to Penny. "So few are here." It was true, hardly anyone was there except us and a group of Russians. "Perhaps now we may have our tea together?" He gave her his most winning smile.

Penny looked bewildered, as if she were trying to

remember Paul's asking her to have tea. She smiled uncertainly at Mr. Kemel. "I am so sorry. Some other time perhaps."

Mr. Kemel bowed, bade us good evening, and left. I felt quite sure that he was angry, although he didn't let it show. I shivered.

My parents left and I finished off the watermelon and got up. Paul was ordering tea.

"Stay for a bit," he said to me, but I know when three's a crowd. He walked to the door with me. "Thank you very much, Hardy," he said. His eyes were very black. "You are a jewel."

While the elevator clunked its way up, I had a refrain singing in my head: *You are a jewel a jewel a jewel.* I had saved my sister from a creepy man, and I had made the man I loved happy at great expense to my own feelings. I was a jewel. I began to wonder what kind of jewel I was. An emerald maybe?

In my room I hung out the window and thought of great warriors riding armored on prancing white steeds to court their ladies, who leaned out their windows in the soft night and tossed one red rose to their heroes. You could really believe all that in Samarkand. Up till now I'd thought of knights and ladies as people in a book, or the little figures Andrew and I used to play with.

The stars looked very close and bright. In their

light, I saw a man walk up the shaded street toward the mausoleum. I thought for a second that it was Mr. Kemel, but this man wasn't limping. I wondered what Paul and Penny were talking about. And then I began to think of Tamerlane's grandson, a good man who hated war. He was a brilliant astronomer. We had been to see his observatory and we had leaned down to look at the enormous iron track that was part of his sextant. He had had his head cut off for trying to find out the truth about the stars. Everybody knows who Tamerlane was, but how many people know the name of Ulugh-Beg?

A rooster with a confused time sense began to crow somewhere in the long row of adobe huts across the street. Then a pack of dogs chased something, a cat or maybe a rabbit, under my window. They barked for a long time. After I went to bed, they were still barking.

I wanted to stay awake till Penny came in, but I didn't make it. It seemed to me that someone as much in love as I was wouldn't be able to sleep or eat, but I was having no trouble at all. I planned to dream about Paul, but instead I dreamed that I was in the big school track meet on the university campus. I was running in the relay and I was ahead, but the runner next to me kept trying to trip me. I looked at him and it was Mr. Kemel. Then my best friend, Allie, threw her javelin at him, and he fell flat. I raced across the finish line shouting, "Virtue is its own reward." I woke up and wondered if it was and went back to sleep.

two

_____

WE WERE all waiting for my father to finish shaving. My mother had been ready since dawn, practically, as she always is. She's learned to carry a book with her at all times to keep from going mad while she waits for the rest of us; the book this time was something by Daphne du Maurier. My sister drooped in front of the mirror studying her makeup the way other people study a great painting. Andrew, pale but no longer green, was watching my father.

My father is probably one of the last living men to

shave with a straight-edged razor. He claims to have sensitive skin. I think he just enjoys the ritual. It takes him forever, but he can't be hurried or, so he says, he'll cut himself. So there he was, his face covered with lather that looked like whipped cream; he was scraping the razor carefully along his jaw and he was singing. Singing is part of the act, and it's always the same two or three songs. Over the years, a listener gets a very distorted version of his songs because he has his face screwed up into peculiar grimaces while he shaves the different parts, so you don't get the words too clearly. Also, my father can't carry a tune. At the moment he was singing "The Sheik of Araby."

"On television," Andrew said, "sheik is pronounced 'shake.'"

My father paused, razor held in the air, and looked at Andrew in the mirror. I have to spell his reply phonetically in order to preserve the full impact of his wit. "My sheek," he said, "is not a chic shake."

Andrew sighed. Penny groaned. My mother looked up from her book and said, "What is it?"

"Dad just made a joke," Penny said.

"Oh." My mother went back to Daphne du Maurier.

Chuckling happily my father scraped his cheek, waved off a dollop of foam, and went back to his song. ". . . a night when *umm* asleep . . ." *Scrape,*

25

scrape, scrape. "... into *um* tent *um* creep ..."

"I've puzzled over that song for years," Andrew said. "I can't see it at all."

"See what?" I said, to pass the time, and also because I'm always interested in what goes on in my brother's mind, which is often astonishing.

"Well, I mean, sheiks don't go around crawling

into girls' tents, do they? A sheik is a big shot, with a retinue and all."

"And a harem," I said.

"Right. He summons girls. He doesn't sneak into their tents. Anyway you can't tell me those girls each had a private tent. The picture is all wrong."

My father shaved his upper lip with great care. Then he said, "In addition to having an unfortunately literal turn of mind, Andrew, you don't know a cussed thing about sheiks."

"Do you?" said Penny.

My father gave her a cold look. He lets us say what we think, but he doesn't like it if we sound impertinent. "I do not need to have experienced the Civil War to enjoy 'The Battle Hymn of the Republic.'" And with that cryptic remark, he shut the bathroom door.

My mother looked up. "I hope he doesn't stay in there too long with the door shut. These Russian bathrooms are really not very clean."

I repeated what Dad had said. "The Russians have never recognized the germ."

"Evil drains," Andrew said.

The phone rang, and Penny leaped for it. You could read her mind: it might be Paul; it might be the English guy she had talked to at the tombs; it might be, God forbid, Mr. Kemel.

"Yes?" Only Penny can make a monosyllable like

"yes" sound like an operatic aria. Then her face fell. "Oh, certainly. One moment please." She put down the phone and knocked on the bathroom door. "Dad, phone."

My mother murmured, "Who could it be?"

"The International Bank," Andrew said. In Moscow our room phones rang constantly with wrong numbers. The rest of us gave up answering, but my mother can't bear to let a phone ring, so she would get into these ridiculous conversations with non-English-speaking people, trying to tell them they had the wrong number. Once after a very frustrating attempt with some woman, the woman managed to say in English, "International Bank." My mother, thoroughly flustered by this time but proper to the end, said, "Madam, are you calling the International Bank or are you he?" That's the kind of thing you never live down in our family.

My father emerged from the bathroom, his face pink from hot towels. "Hello? Hello?—Yes, this is Harlow—Oh yes, Professor Popov." And then he went into Russian.

Professor Popov was a man at the university in Samarkand that my father's dean had met, and Dad had been told to look him up, establish cultural relations and all that. But when we got to Samarkand, the professor had been unavailable, out of town or something.

After quite a bit of chatter my father hung up. "Everybody get ready now. Popov is coming over for breakfast."

"Dad," Penny said, "we've been ready for an hour. Ready and *waiting*."

My mother patted her hair. "What is the professor's field, Harold?" She is a well-trained faculty wife.

"Gorki." My father picked out his best tie. "And Andrew, please try not to ask him what he thinks about Solzhenitzyn."

Andrew had asked that question of a group of Russian students that talked to us in Moscow, and it had been quite embarrassing.

"I don't make the same mistake twice," Andrew said.

"With your gift for boo-boos, you don't have to," Penny said.

I wondered why she was being so mean this morning. Maybe things hadn't gone well with Paul. Not that I wished her any bad luck, but if he got mad at her and looked around him and saw the love shining out of my eyes . . . Love on the rebound would be better than no love at all. Then I caught a glimpse of myself in the mirror and hope vanished. Moonfaced Hardy. And no matter what I did to my hair, five minutes later I always looked as if I'd just come out of a wind tunnel. Instead of my usual jeans, in which at least I'm anonymous, I was wearing a dress and panty hose, out of deference to my mother's notion of what the American image ought to be. The dress was dark blue with a white collar, and it made me look like a fat nun who had lost her convent. My panty hose sagged like old rags; I never can keep them up tight enough. In comparison to the rest of me, my legs are fairly thin—*slender* is the word I prefer—so if panty hose fit me around the waist, they hang in folds on my legs. I had lost my new glasses, which were at least in style, and I had to wear the old ones that make me look like an owl. It was a hopeless situation. My mother said I would slim out in a year or so, but how did she know?—she's been slender and beautiful all her life, and so has Penny. It doesn't seem fair.

"Off we go," my father said.

My mother put her hand on Andrew's head. "Dear, be careful what you eat."

"Don't worry," Andrew said. "Cornflakes and train tea."

But of course when we got there, there were no cornflakes, and he had to settle for unleavened bread, which is kind of good but not if you feel queasy.

Professor Popov came in with gusto. He was a short man with a shiny bald head, a fat tummy and a hearty voice. He embraced my father the way European men do, and greeted us all around with much beaming and bowing.

It turned out that he spoke very little English so most of the time he and my father talked Russian. For courtesy's sake he would now and then bow like mad to my mother and try a little English, like: "Madam, you are pleasant to Samarkand, yes?" My mother said yes, very pleasant. Later he fixed me with his bright eyes and said, "Boring or not boring, which one?"

I hadn't the faintest idea what it was that might or might not be boring, but I followed Mother's example and said, "Oh, not at all." He clasped his hands together and said, "Goot."

He left as noisily as he had come, making a production of paying for our breakfast, although we had more meal coupons than we could ever use up, partly because of Andrew's missing a number of meals.

"He seems a nice man," my mother said when he had gone.

My father was watching him as he left the dining room. He looked thoughtful. "A man full of questions."

"What kind of questions?" Penny said.

My father filled his pipe the way he does when his mind is on something, tamping down the tobacco till you think it must be mush. "He seems not to have heard from the dean. I think he wasn't sure who I was. Or at least what I'm doing here. He didn't seem to understand that our colleges haven't opened yet, that I'm on vacation."

"Not heard from the dean?" my mother said. "How very odd."

"Well, mail *is* slow. Or . . ." He stopped talking to get the pipe lighted. "Or he was double-checking."

"Whatever for?" Mother said.

"Maybe he thinks you're a Trotskyite," Andrew said.

"Anybody can see," my mother said, "that your father is just what he says he is."

My father laughed. "Russians tend to be cautious about strangers. I guess they have their reasons."

"You could be smuggling an anti-Soviet manuscript out of the country," Andrew said.

At that moment, I saw Paul go past the dining room door. I excused myself and headed for the lobby.

He was already walking quickly down the street that led to the market. I had to hurry to catch up with him, but it was not for nothing that I was the hundred-yard-dash champion of Wenham High. Just before I reached him, I slowed down to a casual stroll, although I was breathing a little hard. I started to pass him with my head down, looking very abstracted. When he said good morning, I looked around with a start of surprise. For a second I stared at him as if I couldn't quite place him. Then I said,

"Oh, it's you."

I thought I saw a twinkle in his eyes, but he just nodded gravely and I couldn't tell whether he knew I was chasing him or not.

"Lovely day," he said.

Until he mentioned it, I hadn't noticed, but it *was* a lovely day. I looked at the world as if I were seeing it for the first time. The breeze blowing in from the desert was soft and warm. The last of the autumn leaves were golden and the hills were golden, too. In fact, the town and the whole countryside were all in shades of brown and gold. I wondered why I hadn't noticed it. The only other colors were the blue, green and red doors in the long, brown adobe wall, the intensely blue robe of a tall Mohammedan who walked ahead of us, and through the trees a glimpse of the blue mosaics of some of the mosques and mausoleums. The mosque of Bibi-Khanym, which hasn't been restored, rose up from the hill ahead of us, very gaunt and ruined looking.

"I like that one the best," I said, nodding toward the mosque. There was hardly any blue left on it; it was kind of sand colored.

"Yes," he said. "All that lovely blue gets a bit much, doesn't it. Especially when you've been traveling the mosque route. Bakhara, Irkutsk, and all that."

"Do you like to travel?" I said.

33

He shrugged. "One gets sick of it."

There was a pause, and I didn't know whether to move on by myself or walk along with him or what. I couldn't think of one sensible thing to say. My heart began to pound with embarrassment and I knew I was blushing. He seemed to be thinking of something else, and I was grateful for that. But the silence was getting awful. Maybe if I just dropped behind, he wouldn't notice. I slowed down, but then he looked at me.

"I am walking too fast for you?"

"No, no, I was just . . . I have a pebble in my shoe."

"Ah, let me find it for you."

To my horror, he dropped down on one knee and began to unlace my shoe. "This one?"

"Yes, but I think it's all right now. It must have worked its way out." I felt like the biggest fool in Asia. People were looking at us. Paul pulled off my shoe, and I had to grab his shoulder to keep my balance. His sweater felt nice and woolly. I would have enjoyed the moment if I hadn't been so embarrassed. He held up the shoe and shook it. Nothing, of course, fell out.

"There," he said, "that should do it. Nasty sharp, little stone. No wonder it hurt." He put the shoe back on my foot and laced it up.

"Thank you very much." My voice sounded feeble. I didn't know if he was putting me on or just

going along with my act or whether there really had been a stone I hadn't felt.

"Sorry I was walking so fast. I was thinking out a problem," he said.

"Then you don't want someone tagging along."

"Nonsense. It is very comfortable your being along. It helps me to think." He gave me that smile that reduced me to Jell-O.

"Me?" I said. I was dying to know what he was thinking about but I thought he would tell me if he wanted me to know. I didn't want to be nosy, not with Paul. Anyway it probably had to do with Penny.

"Were you going to the market? Shall we look about?" He took my arm and steered me toward the market, past the long bench, where eight ancient men in robes and turbans looked as if they had sat there in the sun for a thousand years.

Just as we turned in by a long table heaped up with yellow onions, I saw Mr. Kemel. He must have angled in ahead of us, but I had been too absorbed to notice him. He glanced toward the market, but he didn't seem to see us. He went limping up the street.

"Wasn't that Mr. Kemel?" I said.

"Who?" Paul picked up an onion and studied it.

"Mr. Kemel. The Turkish man who's staying at the hotel."

"Oh, that one. I didn't notice."

But he had noticed; I'd seen him look at Mr.

Kemel. Maybe he saw him as a rival, so he didn't like to think about him. Sometimes I pretend unpleasant things don't exist. The only trouble is, they do.

Paul gave me a thorough tour of the market. It was the best outdoor market I'd ever seen, everything separate and clean, a long table heaped up with melons, another with persimmons, one with pomegranates, and so on. Paul bought me some persimmons and pomegranates and a little yellow melon. Then we sat on a bench at an open stall and I had an ice-cream cone and Paul had green tea. It was a lovely morning. I even forgot to be self-conscious. He asked me questions about America, but he never once mentioned Penny. He thought New York was the capital of America.

When we got back to the hotel, he thanked me for a pleasant morning. "You did me, I think, one big favor, Hardy."

"Good," I said.

"Yes. You help me to make a decision. Now I see more clear."

I couldn't resist. "What decision? Or is it a secret?"

He smiled. "Secret, yes. But I tell you this: I was made suggestion . . . what is your word?—offer. Business offer. I now see I must turn down."

I couldn't imagine what I had had to do with a business offer. Probably something about the band.

I was trying to think of a polite way to find out more but just then a big tour spilled into the lobby, what seemed like millions of Germans all talking at once, and tons of baggage. The tour leader, who looked like a Wagnerian soprano, was giving instructions in a voice like a bullhorn. Two plump, blond girls pushed between Paul and me. He stood on his toes and waved at me, and then he left.

Only Andrew was in our rooms. He was lying on his back reading a paperback he'd found somewhere, called *The Scarlet Pimpernel*. He sat up and ate a persimmon, puckering up his mouth.

"They're very good but they make you pucker."

"Bittersweet," I said, gazing out the window. "Like love."

"No, not bitter. Just puckery." He paused. "Are you in love?"

"Yes." I wanted to give a long romantic sigh, but what came out sounded more like a small sob. It was so hopeless. He would never love a fourteen-year-old hundred-yard-dash champion with glasses and a weight problem.

"I guess it happens to people," Andrew said, "but I can't see why. I mean it's so stupid." Andrew always turns his head away when men and women kiss each other on TV or in the movies.

"You're too young to understand."

"Oh, come off it. You sound like Penny."

"Well, there are certain things that are governed by biology and one's biological age . . ."

"Hardy," he said, "you don't know anything about biology."

He was right; I didn't. He was the one who collected frogs and studied weird things under his microscope. He always won a prize at the science fair.

After a minute he said, "What's it like?"

"What's what like?"

"Love." He said it as if he'd just tasted a lemon.

"You already told me; it's stupid."

"No, really, what is it like?"

"I don't know why you want to know. You're above such things."

"A person has a certain scientific interest."

I thought. "Well, it's awful and wonderful."

"That doesn't mean anything."

"Well, you suffer a lot and you're on Cloud Nine a lot . . ." I tried to think how to describe it. "You get very aware of things you never thought much about before."

"Like what?"

"Oh, like sunsets and the moon. Poetry. Love songs."

"Yecch," he said.

"And the color of people's eyes, not just blue or black, but all the little lights they get in them. And the shape of a person's nose . . ." I was beginning to warm up to the subject.

"Anybody's nose or just the nose of the loved one?"

"Just the . . ." I looked at him suspiciously. "You're putting me on."

He grinned. "Well, Sis, it *is* pretty funny."

It's been years since I got mad at Andrew so I just snorted indignantly. He was sitting up on the bed, drawing a picture of a sea gull on the inside back cover of *The Scarlet Pimpernel*. He draws very well.

"I can remember," he said, squinting at his drawing, "when you'd rather stay home and play Knights with me than anything in the world." He looked up at me with an odd expression. "Remember all those little knights Dad brought us from England?"

"Of course I remember." They were wonderful knights and we had built castles and stuff for them and played with them for hours. The leaders were named for the knights of the Round Table. "Remember those battles between Modred and Lancelot?"

"Yeah." He was smiling, but he looked sad. We had always been close, and when he was six and I was not quite ten, or he was seven and I wasn't yet eleven, we didn't seem far apart in age. He was always so bright and in some ways so grown up, always thinking deep thoughts.

"Remember," I said, "the time you heard about

the Black Hole of the Universe, and we stayed awake half the night arguing about what would happen to us if we fell into it . . .''

"We were too scared to go to sleep." He pushed his hair off his forehead. His hair is brown and floppy and it always looks, as my father says, as if he'd slept in it.

"Listen," I said, "if we had those knights here now, I'd give you a challenge to battle that would ring from the ramparts."

"Yeah?" He was still looking at me in that funny way, his eyes bright, almost as if he might cry. He got up from the bed and got his ditty bag. He rummaged around in it and pulled out four of those good old knights. I couldn't believe it. I thought he'd stopped playing with them ages ago.

"I don't play with them actually," he said. "I just keep them around for old times' sake."

Now I was the one who felt sad. I picked up Galahad, with his lovely tin silvery shield and his red coat of arms. He fitted in the palm of my hand, and I had this funny feeling that I was holding my lost childhood in my hand. I set him down and galloped him toward Modred. "Charge!"

Within about twenty seconds we'd both forgotten that we were too old to play with toy knights. I made a castle out of a box from the beriozka shop, and Andrew sketched a beautiful fortress on the cardboard from Dad's shirt. We were having such a good time, we didn't even hear Penny and Mother come in, until Penny said, "Mother! What are those stupid children doing?"

Andrew scooped up the knights so fast, I hardly saw them go. And I said, "We were reconstructing history, if it's of any consequence to you."

"It's bad enough for a big boy like Andrew," Penny said, grabbing my castle, "but a teen-ager . . . And that happens to be my box."

I snatched it back. "It happens to be my castle."

Penny squealed. "Mother! Do something about these revolting children."

My mother was taking off her hat and patting down her hair. She said, "Hardy, take Andrew to lunch, dear, will you. We have eaten. And I think that is Penny's box. Penny dear, don't shriek."

As we lurched downward in the elevator, Andrew grinned at me. He looked a lot happier. "That was just like old times, wasn't it? Penny screaming at us and everything."

I agreed. But when we went into the dining room, I forgot all about the knights and Andrew because I was so busy trying to see if Paul was anywhere around. The old times were really gone.

three

THAT EVENING, Professor Popov and three of his students took us all to the opera. The opera house, which is near the hotel, is fairly new and the four of them were very proud of it. The opera was something adapted from an Uzbek legend, and the music sounded to me very Oriental and strange, but I liked it.

Professor Popov kept time by drumming on his fat stomach with his fingertips, and when he wasn't doing that, he ate sunflower seeds with tiny little clicks of his teeth like a squirrel.

I liked the students very much. There was an awfully pretty girl named Masha, and two boys, Ivan and Pyotr. They spoke very good English and they joked with me a lot. Pyotr was terribly handsome, tall and dark with gorgeous soulful eyes; he was wearing a black silk skullcap embroidered all over with bright red, green and blue designs. If I hadn't already been in love with Paul, I might have fallen in love with Pyotr. He told me funny stories about members of the cast, a little bit mean, actually, but funny. Like how the tenor wore a wig and one night it got swept off when he took off his hat with a big flourish. I don't know if he was making it all up. Andrew and I laughed a lot. There were only eleven other people in the audience, and Ivan said the director hadn't decided until five o'clock whether to give a performance that night or not. It all seemed very relaxed.

Afterward we went back to the hotel for tea and something to eat, except for Andrew, who went upstairs to bed. The Russians stayed a long time and it was very gay. The grownups drank a bottle of champagne, and I had a little of my mother's. I wanted to appear sophisticated, but the bubbles got in my nose and made me choke.

It was a night off for the band, so I could only dream about Paul. I was glad he was not there to see how Penny flirted with Ivan and Pyotr. She has no shame. The three Russians asked a million questions about the United States. It was surprising to me how much they didn't know about us. Masha, too, thought New York was the capital, and she kept asking what things cost. How much did Penny's pant suit cost, how much did my sweater cost, and so on. They didn't believe us, I think; they thought things would cost a great deal more.

My father and Professor Popov jabbered away in Russian, and my mother beamed at us all. She loves music and she had really enjoyed the opera; I think that was what she was still thinking about as she murmured the right answers: "Really" and "How very interesting" and "Of course." She's programmed to say the right thing without having to think about it. It would be very useful to be able to do that.

When we finally left, Mr. Kemel was just coming into the lobby from outside. He looked windblown, although there wasn't any wind. I thought he looked startled when he saw Professor Popov, but the professor just gave him a cold stare. I felt, though, that he recognized him. Mr. Kemel nodded to us and went on up in the elevator.

I popped in to see if Andrew was asleep. He was kneeling by the window in the dark, staring down at the courtyard.

"What's up?" I said.

"There are ghosts abroad," he said.

But just then our parents came in, and that ended that.

In the morning, I got a chance to ask what he'd meant.

"Ghosts."

"Where?"

"In the courtyard, flickering around like fireflies. And out in our corridor, whispering."

"There aren't any ghosts." I said it firmly though I wasn't sure it was true. "You heard people whispering and you saw people with flashlights."

He gave me a pitying look. "Sometimes I think you must have suffered a terrible percussion."

"Andrew, you don't make sense." We went outside and sat down on a bench beside a man wearing a black-and-white skullcap. He looked like the man I had noticed before, but I wasn't sure.

"I make perfect sense. You must have gotten hit on the head and had a percussion to be so dense."

"*Con*cussion."

He shrugged. "Same difference. Anyway there were ghosts. I looked in the hall when I heard the whispering. Nobody was there. And I could see straight into the courtyard. There were just lights." He leaned back and stretched out his legs. "Probably some ghosts wandered in from the mausoleums."

It was warm in the sun, but I shivered. You did

46

begin to get the feeling that the town was dominated by the dead. Even the living seemed to move in a kind of dreamlike way. I stole a glance at the man next to us. He was asleep.

"There goes the Turkish Delight," Andrew said. "And your friend Paul."

I had taken off my glasses to clean them but I shoved them back onto my nose. "Not together . . . Where?"

"Together. There."

I saw them by the door, talking, very intent. Then Paul seemed to jerk away, as if he were physically tied to Mr. Kemel although they were not touching. Paul went through the door and disappeared. Mr. Kemel stood there for a moment and then he went inside too, more slowly, limping even more than usual.

"I didn't know those two were buddies."

"They aren't buddies," I snapped at him. "They can say good morning, can't they?"

"It was a long good morning. Well, if Kemel is Tamerlane, maybe Paul is Ulugh-Beg." He grinned at me. "And he'll get his head cut off." He made a vivid gesture across his throat.

"You're revolting." As we walked away, I glanced back at the man who'd been sitting beside us. His eyes were wide open, and he was looking at us. "I keep seeing that man."

"I know. He watches us."

"Why?"

He shrugged. "Who knows. We're about the only Americans in town, I think."

"So?"

"I suppose they wonder what we're doing here. We're out of season."

As we passed the old beggar who sat cross-legged on the sidewalk, he stopped his muttered spiel and stared at us with black eyes you couldn't see into. Maybe he was too proud to beg from foreigners.

"The vibrations around here are terrible," Andrew said. "When is it we're leaving?"

"Saturday afternoon."

"Anna has asked me three times." Anna was our chambermaid. Andrew can talk some Russian, and the maids always love him. Russian chambermaids are very nice people and they love kids.

In the evening our parents went to a Russian movie. Andrew and I went for a walk up to the big madrasah, the university Ulugh-Beg built. It's just a tourist's point of interest now. It's very beautiful, with big domes and blue mosaics like the mausoleums. It was almost dark and hardly anyone was around. We walked across the grass, which is very uneven and a good place to fall flat on your face, which I almost did, and we tried to imagine ourselves students in the fourteenth century.

When we got tired of that, we walked farther up the road until we came to the Shah-i Zindar complex. The moon was just visible through a thin layer of cloud. A taxi was cruising slowly along and a few people strolled along the sidewalk: a young couple with their arms around each other, an old man with a beard, a couple of younger men in those black caps embroidered with white.

"Where are we going?" I said.

Andrew looked up into the complex. "Let's go up the Street of Dead Town."

I shivered. "It'll be awfully dark up there."

"Oh, come on."

I still hung back, though I wouldn't say I was scared to go. "What for?"

"For the fun of it." He started up the grade that led to the wide steps. I had to follow him. Right away it seemed much darker. The trees shut out light, and ahead of us the mausoleums loomed up like a haunted castle. We began to climb the steep stone steps. There are thirty-four of them and if you count them going up and coming down, and you get the same number, you'll get your wish or something. Or maybe it's if you don't get the same number. Our guide was hard to understand. I started to remind Andrew, but he shushed me.

"Why shush?"

"You'll scare off the ghosts. This place must be

absolutely loaded with them."

"It sure must." We stopped a second and stared up at the dark, narrow path between the two rows of tomb houses. There was certainly a mess of people stashed away up here in their tombs. Tamerlane had built it originally for his teacher, I think, and then he added relatives and friends and whoever. None of the places were as big and impressive as his own mausoleum over in back of the hotel, but it was like a whole community of dead people with tombs of different sizes and shapes, covered with all that beautiful mosaic.

When you're in a spot like that with a true believer like Andrew, it's no good telling yourself you don't believe in ghosts. Your mind may say no, but your nerves say yes. As we started down the cobbled, uneven Street of Dead Town, I could feel the cold dank airlessness of death. I began to breathe hard. "I'm leaving."

But Andrew didn't seem to hear me. He kept going slowly up the path, staring into the thick gloom of the tomb entrances on both sides of him. He was my little brother; I couldn't abandon him. I followed.

As we climbed higher, we were above the level of the treetops, and for a moment the moon shone down on us. But as soon as we started along the street, the mausoleums on both sides of us made deep black shadows. They seemed to lean in toward us. I felt smothered. I thought maybe we could just walk along a little way and then turn back, but not Andrew; he had to go popping right inside all those cavernous tombs. Some of them were empty, as far as you could see, but others had the coffins lying there right where you'd fall over them in the dark.

Some were about the size of a small room; but others were bigger, rooms within rooms, and the coffins in the innermost center. There were always steep stone steps. I remembered the guide had said they were built like that so you would have to bend your knee to Allah even if you hadn't meant to. Even infidels, like us, I guess she meant. Well, I not only bent my knee, I fell flat, in the biggest mausoleum, where several people are buried and I forget who they are. I cracked my shin and it really hurt.

"Andrew, I am leaving," I said firmly, staggering to my feet. "Andrew?" No answer. "Darn it, Andrew, stop listening to all those ghosts and listen to me. We are going back to the hotel. Now, Andrew." No answer. I began to get mad. I couldn't see a thing but I swooped around the inner room of the tomb trying to get my hands on my brother. Nothing but dead air. I tripped over a very small coffin and I remembered something about a child, Tamerlane's niece or something. Poor kid; what a place to end up. "Andrew!"

He was not in there. I made my way out, my hands in front of me so I wouldn't crash into a wall. Of course I tripped up the step on the way out too, but it's easier to fall up than to fall down.

My hand touched the depression in the wall where the guide had said the priest stood, facing east when he prayed. It was raised up from the ground, and just deep enough to stand in if you flattened yourself against the cold stone wall. My hand touched something. Cloth. An arm! I opened my mouth to scream, but a hand was clapped over my mouth.

A voice spoke close to my ear. "It's me." It was Andrew.

I was ready to kill him, scaring me half out of my wits like that. I tried to get his hand away so I could tell him what I thought of his big joke, but he clamped it very tight.

"Stop!" He was speaking very low in my ear. "Someone's here. Hold still."

I still thought he was being funny. I tried to get his hand loose. But just then he went very still, and I heard a sound a few feet away from us. At first I wasn't sure what it was, but then it came to me that it was the soft slap of sandals on cobblestones. I pressed myself back against the mosaics of the wall, as hard as I could, and held my breath.

Two men came up the slanting street, not bothering to be quiet. I suppose they didn't expect anyone to be sightseeing in the tombs at such an hour. I could only see their outlines, even though they passed quite close to us. One was tall, dressed in a dark hooded caftan; the other was shorter, wider, and he was dressed in a suit. As they passed I caught the white flash of stitching on his skullcap.

Although it was startling to see anyone there, it didn't really seem too ominous. I thought Andrew was dramatizing the situation. So a couple of Uzbeks come up to the tombs at night; so what? But even after he took his hand away from my mouth, I didn't move. I wasn't too anxious to call attention to ourselves.

They went into one of the smaller tombs on the other side. It was one of the few that didn't have any mosaic or decoration of any kind on the inside, although it was elaborately decorated on the outside. I remembered my father saying, "It's all outward show, like having a Cadillac and a house in the country."

One of the men turned on a flashlight and propped it up against the low stone coffin. They knelt beside the coffin; we could just make out their shapes in the dim light. I thought at first they were praying, but one of them picked up the flashlight again and beamed it down at the top of the coffin. They were

looking at something. I moved a little so I could see
better. The tall man had a kind of knapsack. He
took a couple of smallish boxes out of it and laid
them on the top of the coffin. The other man took
the cover off one. I thought then that they must be
thieves, taking a look at the booty. It occurred to
me that we had better get out of there. They would
take a dim view of being spied on by a couple of
American kids.

Then the man in the cap moved the flashlight for
a better look, and for a second it lit up the tall man's
face. It was Mr. Kemel. I was so startled, I reached
for Andrew's hand and began to pull him along in
the shadows, running my other hand along the wall.

I felt the loose stone fall before I heard it hit. The clatter sounded booming in that enclosed and silent place. Instantly the flashlight went out.

We stood still, pressed up against the wall. I could feel Andrew's heart thumping. There was complete silence all along the Street of Dead Town, silence in the tombs. Then the flashlight came on again. The small circle of yellow light moved slowly along the wall where we stood. In a minute it would reach us. I pulled a handful of kopeks out of my pocket and threw them as hard as I could up the street. They landed with loud clinks above the tomb where the men were. At once the light turned in that direction, away from us. Hand-in-hand, Andrew and I ran for the steps.

I found myself counting the stupid steps as we flew down them. We were going so fast, if we had tripped or missed a step, we'd probably have broken about twenty bones. Thirty steps, thirty-one, thirty-two . . . Andrew pulled his hand loose from mine and jumped the last two steps. Thirty-three, thirty-four.

The flashlight caught us just as we hit the path to the street. I showed my true colors as hundred-yard-dash champion of Wenham High. I caught up and passed Andrew, and we didn't stop running until we were way down the street.

"Do you think they got a good look at us?" Andrew was out of breath.

"Not really, but I suppose enough to know it was a couple of kids." We were walking very fast.

"American kids." He grabbed my arm. "Look."

Ahead of us a man got into a taxi and was driven quickly away. It was Mr. Popov.

"It's old home week," Andrew said.

I thought about it. "I suppose there's nothing remarkable in Mr. Popov being out at night and taking a taxi." He didn't answer. "You saw who it was up in the tombs?"

"Sure. Tamerlane. Who else?" He flashed a grin at me.

"Be serious. What was Mr. Kemel doing up there?

And in those clothes?"

"Visiting old friends."

We had arrived at the hotel. "I wish you'd talk sense. Was the other one—the man we've seen—the one you said was watching us?"

"I couldn't see. He could have been."

"What are they up to?"

"Oh, Sis, probably nothing interesting. Maybe Kemel smuggles in costume jewelry or something."

But I could see he was doing some heavy thinking.

four

WE WENT into the dining room and ordered tea. I drank it as hot as I could stand it, to stop my shivering. Paul was on the bandstand, but right at that minute I couldn't even concentrate on him.

"I wish I knew what it's all about," I said.

Andrew dumped sugar into his tea. "Just a couple of ghosts."

"With a twentieth century flashlight."

"Who says a ghost has to stay in his own culture?"

"Oh, Andrew, you're too much." Maybe Mr.

Kemel did smuggle in jewels or something. It was none of our business.

The band took a break, and Paul came to sit with us. I was awfully glad to see him.

"What have you two been up to?" he said. "You look as if you've been playing soccer."

That's a great thing to hear from the man you love. I tried to pat down my hair, which was obviously flying all over the place.

"We were sightseeing," I said.

He raised his eyebrows. "At night?"

"We were spying on Tamerlane," Andrew said. But when Paul asked rather sharply what he meant, Andrew laughed and said, "Kidding."

Paul looked as if he wanted to say more, but the bass player was signaling him. "I would like to talk with you more," he said as he got up. "You will be here a while?"

"Andrew ought to be in bed," I said. "My mother will rave."

"Then you stay, Hardy."

My heart leaped up, but then I remembered, I was only Penny's kid sister.

"I'm not going to bed yet," Andrew said. "I want to see what's on his mind."

"Penny," I said.

"What's there to say about Penny?"

"When you're in love," I said, "you just want to

talk about the person."

"Ah, he's not in love with Penny. It's just a little whirl to pass the time away."

Andrew rejects the idea of being in love. But I wondered if he were right about Paul and Penny. Certainly about Penny. She was like the guy in the song, "I'm choosin' who'sn is near," or however it goes.

We went on sitting there drinking tea, Andrew dreaming about his ghosts or the Black Hole of the Universe or whatever he was dreaming about that week, and me dreaming about Paul.

A big party of Russians were in a dining room closed off for private groups. I figured they were local Party big shots, but Andrew thought they were the spirts of Tamerlane's victims. As he pointed out, you could see them through the glass wall, but you couldn't hear them.

At a table near us, three men were getting a little drunk on vodka. One of them came over and gave Andrew a silver ruble. Andrew tried to give it back, so the man showed him a snapshot of a boy about ten. In Russian, he said it was his son.

Andrew said *"Gde,"* which means *where* in Russian. The man said he lived in Stalingrad. He asked what nationality we were, and he looked a little taken aback when Andrew said "American." They always did; usually they thought we were Finns or

Germans. He shook hands with Andrew and bowed to me and went back to his table. He was a nice man, just homesick and lonesome for his son.

I noticed that Paul had kept a close watch while the man was talking to us. And finally, when the band quit for the night, he joined us, but quite a lot of people came into the dining room then, probably from the opera. The manager came over and said something to Paul. Paul shook his head and answered in Russian. They argued for a minute and then the man went away.

Paul shrugged. "He would like us to play forever. We have done enough for tonight. We have a contract." He got up. "Let us take a small walk."

As we went out of the hotel, Andrew said in my ear, "You going to tell him?"

I was afraid Paul would hear him, so I just shook him off. I was curious to find out why Paul wanted to talk to us. I didn't have any illusions about it being my charms that attracted him. Probably he wanted to weep on our shoulders about Penny.

But it was Professor Popov he wanted to talk about. He asked questions: How did we know Professor Popov? What did he teach? Did my father trust him?

Andrew and I looked at each other. "Why wouldn't he trust him?" Andrew said.

We walked past the little stand, where a woman

sold souvenirs and ice cream during the day, and we crossed the street to the mausoleum of Tamerlane. Paul sat on a low wall and swung his heels. It took him a while to answer.

"You wonder, who is this Paul, this drum player, to ask such questions, yes?"

I was about to say of course we hadn't thought that, but Andrew said, "Well, it had crossed my mind."

Paul laughed. I was thinking so hard about what a delicious laugh he had, that I almost missed what he said. "There is a drug ring here."

"No kidding!" Andrew sounded delighted. "Hey, just like TV."

"How do you know?" I said.

He didn't answer. The silence got awfully tight.

Andrew broke it. "You don't mean Professor Popov is in it?"

"It seems unlikely, yes? Very unlikely." Paul was frowning, studying the toes of his boots. "I myself think it is unlikely. And yet I have seen him with someone . . . someone he should not know."

"Mr. Kemel?" Andrew said.

"Kemel!" I hadn't seriously thought of him as that dangerous.

"Yes. That surprises you? He is a Turk, and there is smuggling of drugs from Turkey into the Soviet Union." He paused. "You asked, Hardy, how I know.

Kemel made me an offer. You remember, the day we had our walk . . ."

"Yes. You said I helped you decide something."

"Exactly. Kemel needs someone to take some merchandise to Moscow. His usual system, his messengers, you understand, something has gone wrong; someone is missing or not to be trusted."

"Did you consider doing it?" Andrew has a way of asking the questions other people only think of.

Paul lit a cigarette and threw the match so it made an arc of light, like a firefly. "I was tempted."

I wished I could go away. I didn't want to hear about it anymore. I turned my head away from him.

"Did he offer you a big pot of money?" Andrew said.

"It was not money. I do not care so much about money." He took a long drag on the cigarette, and I was in such a state by this time, I wondered if it was pot he was smoking. "He offered me a passport."

"Haven't you got a passport?" I said.

"Oh, yes. But it will not take me out of Eastern Europe."

I was overcome with relief. This I could understand. Money I could not have forgiven.

He read my mind. "It is not so wicked, for a passport? Yes, it is, Hardy. You can scorn money because you are rich. To others it can mean life or death."

"We aren't rich."

"All Americans are rich." He smiled at me.

"You saw Professor Popov with Kemel?" Andrew asked.

"Yes. And I say to myself, why would a professor at the university of Samarkand know Kemel?" He shook his head. "I would not bother about it; it is of no matter to me. But I worry about you."

"Me?" I said.

Gently he corrected me. "You, all of you. You are my friends."

"You worry about Penny," Andrew said, "because you've got a thing for her. Why didn't you go to the police? Or did you?"

He shrugged. "What could I prove? Kemel never said what his merchandise was. And who would believe me? I am suspect myself; I am a wandering musician. A band player. It is the legend, is it not, that all band players use drugs? They are all . . . what is your word?"

"Junkies," Andrew said.

"So. I would only get myself in trouble. I am no brave man; I dedicate my life to staying out of trouble."

"If Kemel never said what his stuff was, maybe it's not dope," Andrew said. "Maybe it's like Turkish rugs or something."

Paul laughed. "Then he would have said, would he not? Besides, I have seen him with a man, a local man, I know to be in the smuggling."

"How do you know?" Andrew said.

"He sells to one in the band. No, not me. I have vice but not of drugs. Drugs are stupid."

"Why are you concerned about us?"

"I only guess. You go soon to Moscow. He wishes to send a package to Moscow."

"To his connection," Andrew said.

"But he must know we wouldn't carry drugs for him," I said.

"He doesn't know," Paul said. "The price is high. Or he might just ask your parents to deliver a package to a friend."

"We might look inside," Andrew said.

"Unlikely. You are the well-bred Americans who do not sneak, is it not so?"

"I can imagine our parents' reaction if one of us said, 'Let's take a peek at Mr. Kemel's package.' " I said.

"Precisely. Or you know, he might try to get a package into your luggage."

That, of course, was the moment to tell him what we had just seen in the Street of Dead Town, and I was about to, but Andrew nudged me and shook his head. It didn't seem right to do it on my own, till we'd talked it over, although my instincts then were all for telling Paul everything.

On the way back to the hotel, Paul asked Andrew

about the man who had given him the ruble. He seemed satisfied with the story.

"Missing his boy. Russians are sentimental. I have a brother your age. You are perhaps eleven?"

"Eleven next Tuesday."

I had almost forgotten it was so close to Andrew's birthday. I'd have to think of a good present. The year before I'd hidden a tennis racket underneath the shirts in his bureau, and it took him ages to find it.

"Well," I said to Paul, "thanks for warning us. I don't think we have anything to worry about, though, since we're innocent."

He frowned. "In some countries innocence is beside the point."

"What do you mean?"

He didn't answer for a moment or two. "My father believed, like you, in justice, in innocence. In truth. He offered the truth, and he was shot."

"Shot dead?" Andrew said.

Paul nodded. "Dead." He left us in the lobby and walked quickly away.

Andrew and I couldn't say anything in the elevator, because there were two large East Germans crammed in there with us, jabbering away to each other over our heads.

In our rooms, we opened my window and hung out before we said anything. People say Soviet tourist

hotel rooms are bugged, which may or may not be true, but it didn't seem like the time to test it out.

"What did you make of all that?" Andrew said in a low voice.

"Poor Paul." I was thinking of the fate of his father. I felt very sad.

Andrew punched my arm impatiently. "Think, Hardy. Don't emote."

"Think about what?"

He lowered his voice still more. "Is Paul in it?"

I was stunned. "In what?"

"You know. With Mr. K."

"Are you out of your mind?"

"Sometimes. Not always."

"Why would he be telling us all that if he . . . Oh, Andrew, you read too many books."

"He has a thing for Penny. He wants to spare us. K. says use us; P. says no. He warns us; it's the best he can do."

I didn't know whether to laugh or to yell at him. I was saved the need to make a choice. Our parents came home from the movie and made Andrew go to bed. I went to bed myself, in a state of considerable shock. How my own brother could think such wicked things about a man like Paul, who was practically a saint as all the world could see, was too much for me. And was or was not Mr. Kemel running a drug ring?

five

THE FAMILY went their separate ways the next day, my father taking Andrew to some museum, my mother "browsing" as she calls it, and who knew where Penny went. In the afternoon I went for a walk, wishing I would bump into Paul. I wanted to talk to him alone, although I really didn't know what I would talk about. The things I wanted answers to weren't the kind of things you ask your beloved, like: "You aren't really a dope peddler, are you?" Of course I knew the answer. I just wanted to hear him say it.

I walked slowly along the main street to the market. I might as well buy some more persimmons. I wouldn't find good fresh ones like those in the Wenham market. And if I did find any, old Mr. Lighter would be sure to sell me the rotten ones. For a few minutes I strolled along thinking about home. I hated starting school late; you got behind in everything, not just work, but with people, with the news, who was whose friend this year and all that. Of course there were some advantages. I'd have enough topics for themes for the rest of the year. I began to imagine titles. "How I Got Lost for Two Hours in My Own Hotel in Moscow." Kind of a long title, but it was a true fact; that darned hotel held 6,000 people, and I always got lost in it. "How I Flew to Tashkent With a Very Wet Uzbek Baby in My Lap." She wasn't really right in my lap; she was slung in a hammock that swayed like mad about six inches above me. "How I Broke the Turkish–Russian Dope Connection."

Actually the old hometown was going to look very quiet after Russia. Not that Samarkand is not quiet, but it's a different quiet. A stillness, a hush. Part of it is the soft air from the desert. We spent a year in Tucson once, and you felt that kind of air there. But in Samarkand it was more than that; it was more as if the city was caught in a magic spell.

I went into a toy shop just to look around, but the

clerk made me nervous. I was afraid he'd know what I was thinking, which was that they were pretty shoddy toys and overpriced. Everything here seemed that way to me, although it wasn't true all over Russia. In Tbilisi, especially, they had wonderful shops and fascinating things to buy, not just for tourists but for themselves.

I went on to the market. It was very crowded, mostly with women who were filling up their string bags with vegetables and fruit. I picked out my persimmons and started back.

As I went by the teahouse near the market, someone called my name. It was Mr. Kemel. I nearly fell over with shock. He jumped up from his table and came after me. Well, I said to myself, it's been a short life but a merry one. I hereby leave all my worldly goods to Paul, the drummer . . .

"Miss Harlow, save a lonely man. Come have a cup of tea."

Well, I hadn't expected that approach. I tried a feeble excuse about meeting my parents, but he didn't listen. He had me firmly by the arm, piloting me to his table. I decided it was better to go quietly than make a scene. He couldn't get too violent right in front of all these people.

"The green tea is very good here. You will try some?"

"No, really, thank you."

"You prefer mineral water, yes?"

I made a face in spite of myself. Mineral water makes me gag.

"Ice cream? *Limonada?*"

I settled for *limonada*, just so he'd stop pestering.

He put the bottle down in front of me, and then he got a glass. But I preferred the bottle. I've seen how Russians wash a glass with a splash of cold water. On trains there is one glass at the water tap that everybody drinks from, and if you're squeamish, you rinse it out.

Mr. Kemel was studying me, and I was getting very nervous. I expected him either to say, "Why were you spying on me last night?" or to ask me to deliver a small package to a friend in Moscow. But he did neither. Instead he said, "Tell me about yourself."

Under the best of circumstances that stops me cold. What is there to say except that I'm fourteen, overweight, nearsighted, and a dependable runner? I smiled feebly and said, "There's nothing to tell."

"I am sure there is much." But already he seemed to be thinking of something else. "I have just come from tomb of Bibi-Khanym. I find them fascinating, the tombs."

"Yes," I said carefully, "I guess we all do."

But nothing came of that either. Instead, he told me that long, stupid story about Tamerlane's girl bride and the architect that fell in love with her while old Mr. T. was away conquering India. It's such a dumb story. The girl told the architect if he'd build her mosque the way she said, he could give her one kiss. And when the time came, she cheated; she put her hand up so he had to kiss her fingers. But his love was so burning hot, it went right through her fingers and left a red mark forever on her lily-white cheek. How about that? And when Tamerlane came home and sent for the architect, the message was that he had made himself a pair of wings and flown away. I think whoever thought up that folk tale was slightly retarded.

Anyway, Mr. Kemel told the story with great feeling. And then he told me he would tell this beautiful tale to his little girl when he got home. The idea of Mr. Kemel with a little girl he told stories to was a shock. I mean really out of character. I looked at him again. Could Paul be mistaken? Maybe the old boy was perfectly okay. Oh, he might dabble in a little touch of smuggling to make ends meet, but suddenly he didn't seem like Public Enemy Number One, or even Six.

Just to check it out, I asked some questions about the alleged little girl. Age, for instance. Age? She has seven years, I was told. Name? Carlotta. Funny name for a Turk, but its strangeness made it more believable.

It turned out he also had two grownup sons living in Istanbul, and as he walked me back to the hotel, I heard all about them and their children. Just a mushy old family man, this Mr. Kemel.

But in the hotel lobby, as I thanked him for the *limonada* again, he said, "Such nice children, you and your little brother. I hope nothing ever happen to you that is bad."

I said I hoped so too, and I went upstairs wondering if I had just been threatened or if I had just passed an hour with a homesick Gramps.

I found Andrew doing an old *New York Times* crossword puzzle.

"Where've you been?" he said. "What's a seven-letter word for a river in India? You had a phone call."

I thought he was kidding. "Who from? The International Bank?"

"Paul."

My heart did three forward somersaults. "Paul?" I had planned to tell Andrew about Kemel, but I forgot that now.

"Yeah." He bent over his puzzle, filling in spaces.

"Well, what did he *say?* It must have been Penny he wanted."

"No, you." He counted the spaces. "What was the second name of Tiberius, eight letters?"

"Claudius. Andrew, what did Paul say?"

He looked up. "Paul?"

I grabbed his shoulder. "You tell me this minute."

"Why are girls so hysterical? I thought you'd turn out better."

"If you don't tell me this minute . . ." I shook him.

"All right, all right, quit that. He said were you here. I said no. He said when would you be here. I said who knows. He said tell you he called."

"What else?"

"No else. That was it. Except he said *thank you* and *good-bye*."

"I'll call him back." But when I tried to get his room number from the desk, I ran into a solid wall of language difficulty. They couldn't understand what I wanted. I went down to the desk and wrote out his name. "PAUL." I pantomimed drumming. Finally they got it. They called his room. No answer. I guess I seemed agitated because the desk clerks looked at me curiously. I gave up and went back upstairs to wait for him to call again.

I sat down right beside the telephone and waited.

six

I sat by the phone for an hour waiting for the miracle to happen, and
working myself up into such a state of nerves that
Andrew finally moved into the other room because
he said I made him feel twitchy.

I kept trying to think what Paul might have called
me about, and I ran the gamut from a proposal to
elope, to a furious order to stop being in love with
him. But that was silly: he couldn't know how I felt.
Or could he? Did it show?

I turned around to face the mirror, and I studied

myself. I imagined myself looking at Paul; how did I look? Stupid, that's how I looked; like a sick cow. But could he see my feelings in my face? I looked at my eyes, which happen to be green. Did they look all gooey with love? After staring at my own eyes for several minutes, all I could tell was that I felt dizzy. I took off my glasses and my face blurred in the mirror. That's what I really felt like, a big blur. If I were only beautiful like Penny . . .

I put my glasses on again. What could I do to improve myself? I'd never really thought much about how I looked: I just took a shower, combed my hair, put on reasonably clean clothes, and I was ready for the day. Maybe the time had come to start making a production, the way Penny did. It was a disagreeable idea, but if that was what you had to do, then that was what you had to do. Where to begin? The answer was obvious: lose weight. I'd gone on a diet before, but I never lasted long. Nobody insisted, and I hadn't been really motivated. Now I was motivated.

It was a grim thought. I like to eat. And I have a very hard time losing even one pound because I am not soft fat, I am very solid. The track coach had me on a diet once, and after a month I had lost exactly one and a half pounds. She gave up on me because I was running faster than anybody else anyway, mainly because I can keep up a steady pace. I have a lot of endurance. All right, I would go on a diet. Tomorrow. My image stared back at me. Oh, all right, then, today. Now.

In the bureau drawer I had stashed away two large Russian chocolate bars (bitter) and one bag of filled Russian candies (heavenly). I took them out and put them in Andrew's ditty bag. I would skip dinner. Unless my parents carried on too much. If they did, I would just eat chicken soup and tea.

In the drawer where the candy had been, I also had a bag of small stones I'd bought in Moscow; lapis lazuli, carnelian, agate and so on. I had a piece of nylon to string them on but I hadn't done it yet. I decided I would put one bead on the string each day that I had moved toward my objective. My objective: the beautification of Hardy Harlow. Any day that I stuck to my diet, and in every other way possible attempted to improve the original Hardy would rate a stone.

I began to get carried away with the idea of the new Mary Harding Harlow: slim, well-groomed, carefully made up. How would Paul be able to resist me? I got out Penny's makeup. She'd kill me if she knew I'd used it, but I'd just try it out and see how it looked. Then I'd buy some of my own.

It was incredible how much junk there was. I laid it all out on the bureau and read the labels. It seemed like you'd begin with Liquid Color Foundation

Spray. Okay. I shook it up, aimed it at my face and squeezed. Instant disaster. My face was covered with icky foam like shaving cream. It got in my eyes, in my nose, in my mouth. Even in one ear. I tried to mop it off with an Intourist towel but it was drying, caking and streaking faster than I could mop. I looked like a clown.

This would never do. What if I were married to Paul, and he was knocking on the dressing room door saying, "May I come in, darling?" He would be in a handsome scarlet silk dressing gown with a monogram, and he would just have shaved with an electric razor.

"One moment, darling," I said to the mirror. "I'm just getting myself together." I'd have to learn to do all this very smoothly.

I picked up a box of face powder labeled: "The Matte Look . . . The You Look . . . in Translucent Pearl." I gave the mirror my most languishing look, focusing on a point behind my shoulder where my invisible husband waited for permission to enter. "Darling, would you like me as a translucent pearl?"

"You already are my pearl," he'd say.

I patted translucent pearl all over my caked face. It made me look like the full moon on a cloudy night. But nothing to do but carry on now. "The eyes, dear," I said to my shadow husband.

"The ayes have it," he replied. But no, that was

my father's kind of answer, not Paul's. "Your eyes are like twin stars," said Paul.

I smiled a tender smile into the mirror, and I picked up a greasy crayon marked "Emerald Green." I carefully daubed it onto my eyelids right up to the eyebrows. It was exciting; it was like painting by numbers. I picked up an ointment marked "White Highlights." When I'd finished with that, I looked as if I had on white goggles. I thought of calling Andrew in to join in the fun, but the fantasy of my husband Paul in the background was too pleasant to give up.

"It only looks odd because I haven't finished," I told him graciously. Men know so little of these things.

"Of course, my love." But his voice began to fade, and I knew I must hurry before I lost his attention.

"You must be patient, dear," I told him. "Man works from sun to sun, but woman's work is never done." I tried a tinkly, silvery laugh, although it didn't sound quite as I'd expected.

From the other bedroom, Andrew yelled. "Who's in there?"

"Only me," I yelled back. And to my phantom husband I murmured, "He's only a child."

With a brown pencil I lined the crease over my eyes, the way I'd seen Penny do it. Only it slipped a couple of times.

Eye liner next. Wet the brush, it said. I couldn't stop to go into the bathroom, so I discreetly spat. I painted just above the eyelashes, but I couldn't seem to get it straight. My eyes got a very zigzag look. Well, perhaps it would make me look Oriental.

Now for the instant lash. I took the little brush and swept it over the upper lashes. "Like so," I said to my husband. Only something was wrong. The lashes got longer and longer, like a spider web. The stuff matted and my eyelashes got so long, I could hardly keep my eyes open. When I blinked, they left black smudges on my cheeks. I decided to give up on that before my eyelashes reached to my knees. "Just a bit out of practice," I murmured. "I've been cultivating the natural look of late."

"Gilding the lily," murmured my husband, watching me with intense admiration.

"Just one more step, my love, and then we shall be ready for the Metropolitan Opera and a little late supper at the St. Regis." The last thing was painting the lower lashes with a few deft strokes. But it smeared badly.

I sat back and looked at myself, my real self. I was a sight to behold. I doubt if my mother would have known me, or if she would have admitted it if she did. I banished the shadow of my husband. "Later, darling." As long as I'd come this far, I should do something with my hair. In its natural state it resembles last year's hay. As a rule I wear it fairly short, but at the moment I needed a haircut badly. My head looked pretty discouraging.

Then inspiration struck. At the market, Paul had pointed out some girls with a lot of little braids. He told me they had thirteen braids if they were unmarried, two if married.

I combed my hair and started braiding. It took quite a while. Those girls must get awfully bored; I'll bet they start looking for a husband pretty young. Or maybe they leave their hair braided for a week or so at a time. I would.

I had trouble with mine. I couldn't make the braids lie flat because my hair was too short. They stuck straight out from my head. But since I'd begun, I might as well finish.

There were four left to do when somebody knocked at the door. It had to be Andrew. I jumped up and draped myself in my bedspread, holding one arm up like the Statue of Liberty. "Come in," I said.

Nothing happened. "Come in, dumb-dumb. The door's unlocked."

Slowly the door opened. Paul stood there, looking at me in total amazement.

I had three choices: I could faint; I could jump out the window; I could try to carry it off. I opted for number three. Using the same fake voice I'd used to the imaginary Paul in my mirror, I said, "Oh, good evening, Paul. How nice to see you."

He swallowed. You could almost hear him swallow. "Good evening, Hardy."

"You called me earlier, I believe."

"Yes. I did." He was getting a wild gleam in his eyes, as if he might burst out laughing.

Being a laughingstock had not been my plan. "What was it you wanted?" If he'd wanted to take me out, I'd have to pretend this was all a joke. Some game I was playing with my little brother.

At that moment my little brother came into the room. He stood as if he had been turned to stone. Then he yelled. "Hardy! What's the matter with you?"

"What's the matter with you?" I said coldly. Now I couldn't pretend it was a game with Andrew; he'd blown my cover. "Didn't you ever see a girl with makeup on before?"

"Not like that. Not outside the circus." He put his hand to his head. "I think I'm having a relapse. I'm hallucinating." He looked at Paul. "Are you seeing the same hallucination I'm seeing?"

Trying to look grave Paul said, "I think Hardy has been experimenting."

It wasn't easy to maintain dignity. "What was it you called me about?" I told myself he couldn't really see me; it was like a masquerade.

"I thought you might know where Penny has gone.

I was a little worried."

I sat down. I felt as if the whole world had melted into a pool of eye shadow and translucent pearl. I should have known it wasn't me he wanted to see.

"She's out somewhere," I said in my own voice.

"One of the Russians took her to somebody's tomb," Andrew said.

Paul looked relieved. "I see. I understood . . . the man called Kemel . . . I understood he was seeing Miss Harlow."

I stared out the window, trying desperately not to cry. It would be the worst kind of humiliation, and the thought of what it would do to the makeup was beyond imagining. "There's more than one Miss Harlow," I said.

He didn't answer for a few seconds. "You were with Kemel?"

I felt very angry all at once. "He bought me a lemonade. Is that a crime?"

He looked startled. "No, no, no. Forgive me for interfering. It was just that . . ."

I couldn't stop sounding angry now or I'd burst into tears. "Just that what?"

"Hardy, this Kemel, he is not a safe man."

"He seems like a perfectly harmless old duck to me. I think you're letting our imaginations run away with us."

Paul looked quickly at me. Then he turned his

head. Just before I heard it, he had heard Penny's voice coming down the hall chattering as usual.

Before I could collect myself enough to get out, Penny and my mother appeared in the doorway. My mother gasped. Penny shrieked. Paul, whom Penny didn't even look at, gave her one despairing glance and left. I dived into the bathroom and locked the door.

seven

EVERYBODY except Andrew was
mad at me. Penny was absolutely
livid because I'd used her precious makeup, "mucked
it all up," she said. My mother was annoyed because I'd upset Penny and made such a mess and be-
haved in what she considered to be a childish and
irresponsible manner. My father was mad because I
stayed in the bathroom so long and used up all the
towels trying to get the guck off my face. In the end
they all went off to dinner without me. It was supposed to be a punishment, but actually it was a re-

lief. In spite of scrubbing my face practically raw, I still had a faint pearly glow punctuated by dots and dashes of green and black eye makeup. It would have been hideously embarrassing to appear like that in the dining room, especially if Paul showed up. I didn't want to face Paul under any circumstances. I couldn't understand why I had been so rotten to him.

My mother worried a little about my missing a meal, but my father said I had enough stored-up fat to last me a month; "like an Eskimo," he said. And "blubber," Penny added. Andrew slipped me a dusty piece of bubble gum out of his jacket pocket, but that was all he could do.

After they had gone, I sat in front of the dressing table again, using just a dab of my mother's face cream to get off the last of the mess. I was chewing Andrew's bubble gum, and when a fairly good-sized bubble collapsed all over my chin, that was the end. I was just doomed to disaster; no point in trying. I got the Russian candy out of Andrew's ditty bag and ate half of it. Then I ate the other half. And right away I felt even worse. Not only was I a complete failure, I didn't even have any character. Now I wouldn't be able to start my necklace of semiprecious stones.

I got the box of stones out of the drawer and laid them out in a row, trying to decide which one I'd string first if I ever showed enough willpower to deserve my necklace. I got it down to a choice between the lapis lazuli and the carnelian. What I really wanted was some amber. I've never seen amber anywhere else, but the Russians go in for it. It's very pretty; kind of golden-colored, like the whole city of Samarkand. I decided I'd start with the carnelian. Maybe tomorrow. Because already I was beginning to think of a new start. If I didn't take myself in hand, nobody else would, except to give advice I couldn't follow. I'd have to be responsible for me. All right. I'd be responsible for me.

In the morning, before the others were even awake, I'd go out and run. If I ran faithfully every day and, most important of all, watched my diet, something might begin to happen. I got out a laundry list and on the back of it I began a list of what not to eat. It's not easy when you're traveling, but I'd made that an excuse; now I'd make it a challenge. No more unleavened bread, no more butter (which would make Dad happy; the Russians charge extra for butter), no dumplings in the soup, no pancakes, no pudding, no candy. I wondered how long a human being could live on tea, because that was about all there was left. And cabbage. I hate cabbage, but if you're going to make a great stride forward, you have to be prepared for sacrifices, trials and tribulations.

I heard someone in the other bedroom. I wondered if Andrew had come back early, maybe his stomach in revolt again. I said, "Andy?" There wasn't any answer, but I could definitely hear someone moving quietly around. I thought it was probably that person, whatever she's called, who snoops in tourists' rooms when they're out. In Moscow, Andrew used to lay traps for her. He'd put a wide rubber band around his trip book, just even with the letters on the cover, and she never put it back the same way. On the last day we were there, he wrote in his book:

I hope you have enjoyed reading my journal. Normally I charge for this, but in your case please accept it free with my compliments. *A. Harlow.*

And that was the day I happened to walk in when she was reading it. It didn't faze her a bit. She smiled and said "Good morning" and put it back on the table. She spoke good English—I guess they'd have to—and she was really a nice girl. It's just her job, I suppose.

I decided to surprise this one. I walked on tiptoe through the bathroom, but I stepped on the heel of one of Andrew's shoes and it made a ploppy sound. I stood still and listened, but I couldn't hear a thing. I flung open the bedroom door, but no one was there. The door to the hall was slightly ajar. I opened it quickly and looked into the hall. The only person there was a man in a dark suit and a black-and-white skullcap, who was walking rapidly toward the elevator. Maybe it was one of Andrew's ghosts. I went back into the room and locked the door with the big clunky key. You're supposed to turn them in at the floor desk, but my family are great key-forgetters.

I thought about that man in the hall. You just didn't see Uzbeks wandering around the floors. Of course he might have come to see about the bedside lamp, which hadn't worked since we'd been there. I tried the lamp; it still didn't work. Just to be sure, I felt around in my parents' suitcases for any strange package. There was nothing. Andrew's ditty bag was left on the floor, the drawstring pulled loose, which was a little unusual. Andrew is compulsively tidy about his personal belongings and especially that ditty bag. He keeps his most private things in it, like the knights. But there was nothing in it that didn't belong there, as far as I could tell. Maybe I had scared the man off. Or maybe we were all getting carried away over nothing. The whole thing seemed like a bad TV show.

When Penny came back, I was prepared for a battle about the makeup, but she was unexpectedly nice. She can be like that, an absolute witch one minute and nice as pie the next. She was going out with Pyotr. When I said, "What about Paul?" I thought she was going to say, "Paul who?", she looked so blank. But she just muttered something and went on applying her lipstick. Lipstick. I'd forgotten about that when I did my great makeup job. Oh, well, the natural look, I always say.

My parents went out shortly after Penny left. My father was still grumbling because he'd had to pay twelve kopeks for a couple of clean towels, but his mind wasn't really on it. They were going to the university for a language department reception. They hadn't expected all this attention from Professor Popov, and my mother was worried about not having the right clothes.

"For the love of heaven, Mary," my father said, "you are not going to be presented to the czars. Modern Russians don't get all dolled up."

"If I only had my white gloves," she said.

My father rolled his eyes like a man having a fit.

"You can borrow my red mittens, Mom," Andrew said, ever helpful. No one knew why Andrew had brought his mittens in September, but he kept saying Russia was a frozen wasteland. I think he had expected to travel by troika pursued by mad wolves frothing at the mouth.

At last my father got my mother on her way, and Andrew and I were left alone. I told him about having heard someone in the room. He checked his journal.

"No signs of tampering here." He looked at the ditty bag. "I did leave this closed, though. I always do."

"It was probably the Snoop," I said.

"Could have been. Or somebody trying to plant a package and you scared them off."

"Whoever it was, nothing seems to have happened." We let it go at that, but I couldn't get it out of my mind.

eight

*V*ERY EARLY, before daylight the next morning, I heard someone get up in my parents' and Andrew's room. I thought it must be Andrew. At first I didn't get up. But when I heard whoever it was go out into the hall, curiosity got the better of me. I got up and dressed in the dark so as not to wake Penny, who had come in late.

When I pushed the button for the elevator, the floor woman reared up from her cot and peered at me sleepily. She said something in Russian or Uzbek or something, and I said, "Good morning," although it was still dark.

When I got out of the elevator, at first I couldn't see anyone except the desk clerk, who was dozing. The lobby was dark except for one dim light. Then, instead of Andrew, I saw my mother. I was really startled until I remembered she'd mentioned getting up early to hear the muezzin at the mosque chanting his morning prayers: "There is no other god but Allah" and all that. I thought Dad had talked her out of it, but apparently not.

A man came in from the street and began to talk to her. I didn't recognize him, and I thought probably she had asked for a taxi to take her out to the mosque. I watched them. He was kind of a seedy-looking man in a dark suit and no hat. He had a round, fat face, and he was smiling at my mother and talking so quietly I couldn't hear anything but a murmur. Then I heard my mother say the one thing, besides good morning, that she knows in Russian, which is: "I don't speak Russian." My father has tried to teach her, but she is like me in regard to languages; we are tone deaf.

He said something else. He seemed very earnest, and he stood close to her. I saw the desk clerk rouse up, look at them for a moment, and then doze off again. Nobody else was in sight.

In English my mother said, "I'm so sorry. I don't speak German either. I'm afraid I'm not very good

at languages. Are you the man from the taxi?"

The man gave a soft little laugh and smote his brow. He spoke again.

"*Oui*," my mother said in her terrible accent, "*je parle français*. A little. *Un peu*. Slowly, you know." She listened to him and shook her head. "You are too fast for me. I'm so sorry. Is it the taxi? I'm ready. *Je suis prête*."

He bowed and took her by the arm. I did a double take. Taxi men don't take you by the arm. I walked toward them. Their backs were to me now. My mother gently removed her arm; I think it had struck her just then that something was odd. All I could think of was the drug bunch.

But as I came up behind them, I heard him speak in French, and although I speak it like a barbarian, I can understand it pretty well. What he was doing, very politely and in three languages, was propositioning my mother.

"Mother!" I spoke loudly, and I caught up with them. "Mother, where are you going." And just to make sure he got it, I said, *"Maman, où allez-vous?"* I forgot till afterward that you don't address your mother in the polite form.

He got it. He gave me one startled look and dropped my mother's arm, which he had retaken. *"Pardon, Madame,"* he said to my mother. *"Mille pardons. Pardon, Madame, pardon."* And bowing a mile a minute he backed out the door.

"Il n'y a pas de quoi," my mother called after him. She looked totally confused. "Hardy dear, I couldn't understand that poor man. He must have been asking directions. I do hope he's not lost at this hour."

I began to laugh. I couldn't help it. "Mom," I said, "he isn't lost. He was propositioning you."

She stared at me. "What?"

"You know, propositioning. 'Come wiz me to de Casbah' and all that."

My mother blinked rapidly. "You mean he was making improper suggestions?"

"In three languages."

"Oh, Hardy, you must be mistaken. I mean at my age . . ."

"I'm not mistaken. Do you want a literal translation?"

"No, no," she said hastily. She stared out the door. "I thought at first he was the taxi; I almost went with him." She began to look a little pleased with herself. "Nothing like that has happened to me in . . . I don't know when. At my age!"

"Well, you see, you're still a charmer."

She smiled thoughtfully, and for a second I saw the self she was looking at, the young, pretty, premarried Mary Harding. I felt sad all of a sudden.

"Don't tell your father," she said.

"Why? Would he be insanely jealous?"

She frowned at her gloves. "He'd laugh." Then she shook it all off in the way she could dispose of things, and she said, "Are you coming to the mosque with me?"

"Well, not unless you want me to." I saw a taxi pull up outside, and the driver get out. He was a young Russian-looking guy that we'd had once before. He didn't seem in the least sinister. He came in, grinned his buck-toothed grin, and held the door for my mother. "Will you be all right?" I called after her.

"Of course." She looked amused at the question. She waved and was gone, Mrs. Harlow, the Russian language professor's wife, née Mary Harding.

I curled up in a corner of the couch to do some serious thinking while nobody was around. I had to think about Andrew's suspicions about Paul. In terms of circumstantial evidence maybe you could make a case against him. We had seen him talking to Kemel; he had cultivated our friendship; he had gone out of his way to make us suspect Kemel and Professor Popov.

But then on the other hand: I thought about those honest eyes; that splendid nose; the way he treated us. It was impossible; he could not be a crook. Not Paul. It didn't matter that we didn't know his last name or even what country he was from. He was my dream man and he had to be honest. I sat there a long time thinking, dozing and waking again.

The door opened, letting in a thin streak of light. The desk clerk opened one eye and went back to sleep again. A man in a dark caftan and a white turban, a tall man, came across the lobby in a long, silent stride. I was so sleepy, I would hardly have noticed him, except that somewhere in my mind I took note of an incongruity: you didn't see Muslims in an Intourist hotel. I looked again. It was Mr. Kemel.

I don't think he would have seen me at all; one wouldn't expect anyone to be sitting there at that hour. But when I saw who it was, I gasped. It's a good thing I don't want to be a spy; I'd always give the show away. He looked at me sharply and stopped. In that moment my mind registered another fact: he had not been limping.

"Good morning," I said.

"Good morning. You are up early." He did not look charmed to see me. Nor did he any longer look like a doting Gramps.

"So are you. I didn't realize you were a Mohammedan, Mr. Kemel."

"Oh, quite." He was trying to pull himself together. He gave me a sick smile. "Not as good a one as I should be."

I thought to myself, I'll drink to that, but I said, "Have you been out to the mosque for the service?"

"Yes," he said. "Exactly." He seemed to be about to go but he hesitated. I wondered what he was going to do about the limp.

"My mother went, too," I said. "Did you see her?"

He looked really startled. "Why, no, actually, I didn't. We must have missed each other."

"Yes, I expect it was crowded." I would have been surprised if there were more than two dozen people there, but of course I knew I could be wrong.

He nodded and went to the elevator. He limped ever so slightly. I was terribly tempted to say I was glad his leg was better, but I restrained myself.

After he'd gone, I decided I might as well get in a spot of self-improvement while everyone was still asleep. I went out and jogged down Gorki Street. Only a few people were out; a couple of young boys who yelled something at me, an old man in a donkey cart, and several other old men in white caftans. So, I thought, we are back again to Mr. Kemel as Up to Something. Mr. Kemel as Fishy Character. He was going to a lot of trouble about whatever it was. Was it drugs, after all? I should have known Paul would be right.

I could hardly wait to talk to Andrew, but he was impossible when he first woke up; he always agreed with everything you said to him and later he didn't remember any of it. Besides, I had to do a conscientious run if I was going to add a bead to my necklace. I turned right and ran hard for several blocks; then right again, and back down the main street to the hotel. I wished I'd packed a sweatshirt. Maybe I could borrow one from Andrew.

I came into the hotel puffing like a fat old man. I was really out of shape. No wonder nobody fell in love with me. The Intourist people were beginning to show up, and they looked at me in surprise.

The one who had been our guide said, "Anything is wrong?"

I felt silly. I shook my head and said, "Just exercising."

They looked at each other. Crazy Americans.

My mother had come back. My father was looking at her sleepily while she told him how interesting the service had been.

"They didn't stone you?" he said.

"Oh, Harold," she said.

"Well, isn't it customary to stone infidels?"

I said, "Did you see Mr. Kemel there?"

They all looked at me in surprise, including Andrew, who was brushing his teeth.

"Mr. Kemel? No. I don't believe he is a Muslim. Or is he? I never thought."

"He doesn't seem the type," my father said.

"He says he is," I said. "I saw him this morning. He said he'd been to the service." I paused and looked at Andrew. "He was wearing a caftan and a turban."

Andrew blinked. He was holding his toothbrush still, up against his front teeth, and he was very foamy at the mouth. "Kemel?" he said.

"Mr. Kemel," my father said automatically. "Watch your manners."

"Maybe you just didn't see him," I said.

My mother looked puzzled. "I would have seen

him. There were only a dozen people there. He must have gone to some other mosque."

"There isn't any other mosque," Andrew said, "except the dead ones."

My father said, "Andrew, kindly close the bathroom door, and conduct your ablutions in the privacy for which they were intended. The sight of you puts me in mind of mad dogs, and that is no image with which to start a new day."

Andrew closed the door, Penny woke up in the other room and yelled at Andrew to close the other door. My father yawned and got up. It was our next to last day in Samarkand.

nine

I WONDER what mosque Mr. Kemel did go to," my mother said at breakfast. "If there's another working one, I'd love to see it. That place this morning was so peaceful and lovely; I really got a lot out of it."

She had thought of it because we had just watched Mr. Kemel come in and sit down at a table near the door. Although he gave no sign, I was sure he had seen us.

"I'll go ask him," Penny said.

"You will not!" Andrew and I said it at the same time.

Penny stared at us. "I don't believe it. Did you say I would not?"

"We did," I said.

"And when did you two take over my actions?"

"Penny," I said, "we have reasons. Let it go at that."

"Has Andrew proved that he really is Tamerlane?"

I knew we were going to have a problem here. Telling Penny not to do something—especially if it's us who tell her—is like waving the old red flag. I gave my mother an imploring look. She looked curious.

"What is wrong with Penny's speaking to Mr. Kemel, dear?"

My father was eating his unleavened bread and studying Mr. Kemel's profile. He hadn't said anything.

Even if I'd wanted to tell them about our suspicions, it would have been hard to pin anything on Mr. Kemel just then; impossible, in fact. And I knew how they'd react: my father believed in the innocent till proven guilty theory and he'd have popped right over and asked Mr. Kemel if he was a drug trader or not. Mr. Kemel would say, "My dear sir, you must be making joke," smile his most plausible smile, and split the scene. My mother would simply refuse to believe it because Mr. Kemel had been so "pleasant." Penny wouldn't believe anything Andrew or I said.

I said, "Well, I happen to have been told on good authority that . . ." I stopped. "I can't tell you right now, but it's better not to get involved."

Penny scoffed. "You don't even know anybody to talk to. How could anyone . . ." She looked at me sharply. "Was it Paul?" She didn't wait for an answer. "It was Paul. Well, Paul is a big bore."

I began to shake with rage. "He is not."

"I thought you were in love with him," Andrew said.

"Don't be a baby," Penny said. "What do you know?"

"I shared Andrew's view, with modification," my father said. "I thought you were at least interested in Paul."

"Well, I'm not." Penny looked cross. She hated to be in the wrong in any way. "He's too jealous."

"Poor Paul," my mother said.

"Jealous of Kemel?" my father said. He frowned. I could see he was thinking of Kemel for the first time as a man too old for Penny, not just someone we swapped pleasantries with in the hotel dining room.

Penny read his mind, too. "Of everybody who speaks to me. The Russian students, even Professor Popov, for heaven's sake."

My father said, "Penny, I hope you aren't going to turn into a flirt."

"Turn into!" I should have kept still, but I was busy defending Paul. "She's been a flirt all her life."

"Oh, be quiet," Penny said. "You're just jealous yourself. You've got a crush on Paul."

"I have not." I felt myself turning bright red. It's such a terrible handicap, blushing. People laugh.

My father laughed. "Old Hardy? She's not ready for that nonsense yet."

My mother gave me a thoughtful look. Andrew kicked me under the table.

"Anyway I'm going to ask Mr. Kemel about the mosque," Penny said. She pushed back her chair.

I grabbed my mother's hand. "Don't let her."

"But I'd like to know," Mother said.

I had to stop her. It simply would not do to have Mr. Kemel think we were checking up on him all the time. "Mother," I said, looking her hard in the eye. " 'Mille pardons, Madame. Pardon, Madame.' "

She got it at once. She knew I was blackmailing her; I was threatening to tell about the man who propositioned her. She said quickly, "I'd rather you didn't, Penny. Under the circumstances."

Penny was furious. "What circumstances?"

"I'd just rather you did not."

"This is ridiculous. Just because those interfering children said . . ."

"Sit down, Penny," my father said. He always backed up my mother, even if he didn't know her reasons. "Finish your breakfast."

"But I demand to know," Penny said.

He interrupted her. "You are not yet old enough to make demands of that kind. If your mother wants to discuss it with you, she'll do it in her own good time."

Penny sat down, sulking like mad. In a minute Mr. Kemel left the dining room.

My father suggested that if one or both of us could not stop glaring at each other, Penny and I should leave the table. She stayed. I left. I really didn't feel like squabbling with Penny.

As I went through the lobby, Mr. Kemel materialized from behind a newspaper. I got the feeling he was lying in wait for me. I nodded and tried to hurry past him, but he was right there beside me.

"Miss Harlow," he said in a low voice, "I have urgent question to ask of you. May we sit outside for a moment?"

"I really have a lot to do," I said. My voice sounded squeaky and childish. Adults really do have an unfair advantage. For one thing they're so tall. Especially Mr. Kemel. It's hard to look way up at somebody and sound authoritative.

"I do beg your pardon for my intrusion. It will only take a moment." Somehow he had maneuvered me out of the hotel and around to one of the more inconspicuous benches. He leaned toward me, look-

ing all earnestness and sincerity. "You will recall I mentioned to you my little daughter."

"Yes."

"I have, as you say, a problem." He spread his hands out and gave me what I think is known as a quizzical smile.

"Really? I wish I could help but I really . . ." I started to get up but he began to talk so fast and seriously, I had to listen.

"I did not tell you that my daughter is now living in Moscow."

"No, you didn't." I wondered if there was a daughter.

"Her mother left me and took my child."

"Oh, that's too bad." I was thinking that it was her child too, and I was also thinking that I didn't want to hear about Mr. Kemel's domestic troubles.

"My wife is Russian. I see you were wondering."

I wasn't wondering at all. I just wanted to get away from him. "What is it you want of me, Mr. Kemel?"

"I have something I want to get to my child. I am going to ask you, out of your great kind heart, Miss Harlow, if you would deliver a package to her aunt, who will meet your plane in Moscow."

Well, there it was, just the way Paul had said. I should have split for the hotel right then, but I was half scared, half intrigued. I was curious to see how it was done. I remembered that title for a theme: HOW I BROKE UP AN INTERNATIONAL DOPE RING. "What is it you're sending her, if I'm not too curious?"

He didn't bat an eye. "Not too curious at all, Miss Harlow, especially since you are so kind as to be my courier."

"Oh, wait," I said. "I didn't mean that . . ."

He ignored the interruption. "I am sending her my own dear mother's necklace, which she in turn inherited. The child should have it."

"Why don't you take it to her?"

"I was unable to get a visa for Moscow." He smiled rather sadly. "We Turks are not as welcome as you rich Americans."

I started to say we weren't rich, but I'd already said that. "You could mail it to her."

"I thought of that." He stopped talking until one of the Intourist girls went by. "It is too risky. You see . . ." He lifted his shoulders. "I did not declare it at customs."

"Why not?" I'd forgotten to be scared. He seemed like such an ordinary man now. "Is it very valuable?"

"More than I would care to lose. And there is the sentimental value. I did not declare it because there would have been problems."

I could accept that. Russian customs rules are

fairly complicated. "I might lose it. I wouldn't want the responsibility."

"Miss Harlow, I have observed you carefully. You are a trustworthy young woman. I trust you implicitly."

Trying to get out of it gracefully, I said, "Well, I'd have to ask my father."

"I must ask you, mention it to no one until you are out of this country. No one at all, Miss Harlow. Your father will understand. When you are safely home, and I too, I shall write him and explain of what great service you were to me." He was watching my face. "And there will be a suitable gift to express my gratitude." When I didn't answer, he said, "And for your brother also. What is your brother's greatest desire?"

"A microscope," I said. "The kind that costs about three hundred dollars." That'll stop him, I thought.

But all he did was make a note on the back of an envelope.

"Mr. Kemel," I said, "did one of your men try to plant a package in my brother's luggage?"

He looked pained. "What does this mean, 'plant'? Surely, Miss Harlow, you joke . . ." And then without waiting for an answer, as if I'd said something too silly to pay attention to, he said, "And for you I shall reserve the pleasure to choose something I hope you will always treasure." He kept glancing up at the people who came and went. "I will let you know, Miss Harlow, where to meet me to receive the package I speak of . . ." He stood up unexpectedly.

"Wait a minute." I began to feel scared again and a little angry at being pushed. "I can't possibly do this. I really cannot take the responsibility. I'm sorry."

He began to walk away. Over his shoulder he said, "I am watched. We are all watched. I will get word to you, Miss Harlow. You will not regret." And he was gone, limping off down the street. The Tamerlane limp, I thought. A good disguise.

I looked behind us to see what he had seen, but there were only a pretty young woman with a baby slung over her shoulder, and behind her rolling along like a small boat in a heavy sea, Professor Popov. He waved to me and went on by.

ten

OF COURSE I told Andrew the whole story the minute I could get him alone. I got him out of the room on the pretext of shopping for Mother. She had mentioned a piece of embroidered blue cloth that the woman at the kiosk near the mausoleum had, so we went over there. On the way I told him that Mr. Kemel wanted me to take a package to Moscow.

Andrew gave a long, low whistle. "You're kidding."

"I don't kid about life-and-death matters."

"Life and death? What do you mean?"

"Oh, I just mean it's too serious to joke about."

"Start at the beginning. Tell me everything, including tone of voice and manner, furtive, sneaky, bold, or whatever."

I was up to the part about the mother snatching the little girl off to Moscow, when we got to the kiosk. Andrew waited impatiently while I tried to make the girl behind the counter understand what it was I wanted.

"Why can't Mother ever buy what she wants when she sees it?" he muttered.

"She has to mull it over." I leaned across the counter to point out the cloth I meant, and I knocked a little doll onto the floor. By the time I finished apologizing, Andrew intervened to use his Russian on the girl. She understood him. She came up with the right cloth.

"Now," he said, pulling me along before I'd even counted my change, "tell me the rest."

We sat down on a bench in the shade, across the street from Tamerlane's mausoleum. I found myself checking on the people who passed us, wondering if we were being tailed. I finished the story.

Andrew sat still for a few minutes, thinking hard. Finally he said, "Well, meet him wherever he says, and then we can turn the whole thing over to the police."

I stared at him. "Meet him alone in some spooky rendezvous?..."

"Who said alone? I'll be there."

I looked at him and I would have laughed if he hadn't been so serious. My protector, four feet eleven, 108 pounds ... "You're not supposed to know anything about it. Nobody is."

"But I do know. Don't worry. I'll keep out of sight. And, see, I'll be a witness."

"Andrew, you don't seem to understand. This is not the Scarlet Pimpernel."

"Of course not. It's 1974."

"You're suggesting we go to the police with what is very possibly a box of dope, and we say, 'Hey, guys, look what we've got!' *We* would be in possession. Do you know what the penalty is in Russia for possession of dope?"

"No. Do you?"

"No, but I'll bet it's like fifty years at hard labor."

"But we tell them, this guy gave it to us. To you."
It was hard for him to keep on the outside of the action and to admit it was my caper, but he was trying to be fair.

"Why should they believe us?"

He was exasperated. "Why else should we go to them?"

"They might think Dad was the smuggler. Remember what Paul said about his father telling the truth? And remember what happened to him?"

"Oh. Yeah." Andrew looked scared, and I knew I'd gotten through to him. After a minute he said, "You said, 'what is *possibly* a box of dope.' Do you mean you think it might really be just a necklace?"

"Andy, I don't know. But even if it is, that could be dangerous, too. It's valuable, and he smuggled it in."

"I wonder if that's what he was showing his chum up there on the Street of Dead Town."

"If he was, there's more to it than a present for his daughter."

"Maybe this woman who's going to meet you is a fence."

I grabbed his arm and shook it. "Not 'going to meet me.' Listen, Andrew, nothing is going to be done or said about this. Nothing. Got it? When we're home and safe and it's all far away, we'll tell the family. But for now we just pretend it never happened. Got it?"

He ran his hand through his floppy hair. "I've got it. But it seems a shame, a really swinging adventure like this, and we just act like it never happened."

"Well, that's how we act. Come on, let's go home. I've got to pack."

And I did pack, which was a good thing as it turned out, because I certainly didn't have much time for it later. By the time I'd finished, I was practically falling down asleep. After all I'd been up since before dawn, and about a month's worth of things seemed to have happened since then. I lay down intending to sleep for about ten minutes. In less than twenty-four hours, I was thinking, we'll be on our way home, and all this will seem like a dream. I wondered how whoever it was that was supposed to get the package from me would know who I was. Because no doubt she would meet the plane anyway, not knowing that I'd turned down Mr. Kemel. I wondered how he'd gotten in touch with her after he decided on me. Phone, I suppose, but he'd certainly have to use a code or something. Hotel phones were bugged and probably the pay phones near the hotel. My father says the Russians have always been suspicious of foreigners all through their history. I was thinking about Catherine the Great, a foreigner herself, when I fell asleep.

I half woke up when my mother gently shook my shoulder. I was so tired, it was really painful to try and wake up.

"I'm sorry, dear," she said. She looked very vague to my sleepy eyes. "We are all going to have dinner at the university. I'm sure you'll enjoy it."

I groaned. "Mother, I can't. I'm too tired. I've been up since dawn. Before dawn." I heard her murmuring something to Dad, but I fell asleep again. Then I woke up enough to feel her putting the blanket over me.

"You get a good rest, dear," she said. "I don't think we'll be too late."

"Andrew," I said, rousing up for a minute. "Is Andrew going with you?"

"Yes. For a while anyway. He doesn't want to, but I think he should."

They were just going out the door when I said, "Don't let Andrew come home alone . . ." But the door was already closing. I tried to get up and go after them. I was afraid Kemel would try to talk Andrew into something, and I didn't want him bothering my brother. But I can always find a way to convince myself there's no need to get up when I'm terribly sleepy. I went back to sleep.

When I woke up again, it was dark. After a minute, I turned on the light and saw the note. It was in a sealed envelope, one of those tan envelopes that look like thin wrapping paper that you see in Europe. It was propped against my lamp with no name on it. I thought mother must have come back to tell me something. I tore it open and read the strange handwriting. I read it through three times. It said:

Tamerlane's Tomb. Nine.

I jumped up and checked the doors. As usual my family had left them unlocked. The keys were on

the bureau. I opened my door and looked out. Down the hall, a little way, the man in the black skullcap leaned against the wall, his back toward me. No one else was around. He didn't turn to look at me.

"Listen," I said, louder than I meant to. "You tell him the answer is still no. *Niet, niet, niet.*"

He never turned around. He just walked away and in a minute I heard the heavy door to the fire stairs slam shut. I went back into my room and locked both doors. My hands were shaking. I was scared, and I was mad. How dare that man try to bully me into being his errand girl? I had already told him no. And how dare he send that goon into my room when I was asleep? The idea really shook me. He must have waited till the family left and then sneaked in. Anything could have happened. I was going to have to talk to my family about locking doors. If they had been there, I'd have told them the whole story. I was too scared not to. But as it turned out, it would be hours before I saw them.

A little later there was a knock at my door. I began to shake again. At first I just kept still, but when the knock came again, I said, "Who is it?"

It was only Anna, the maid. My mother had probably asked her to check up and see if I was hungry or anything. Anna was very maternal. I said, "I'm sure glad it's you," which she didn't understand of course but she smiled and chattered away to me in Russian. We always talked to each other in our own language. Only Andrew and my father could talk Russian to her. One day she told Andrew to keep working on his Russian because the Soviet timetable called for taking over America in two years. She seemed to think we would be pleased.

When she was gone, I locked the door again. Since the family was gone, I'd skip dinner. That would help toward my necklace. Necklace! I shuddered. Maybe I'd change it to a bracelet.

When it was a few minutes before nine, I decided to go down to the dining room for some soup. I was really starving, and also I was not anxious to stay in the room as the time came when I was supposed to be meeting Kemel at the tomb. The whole thing made me very nervous. Besides, Paul would be in the dining room.

I put on a clean blouse, gave my hair a combing, and cautiously checked the hall. The floor clerk wasn't at her desk so I left the keys there, which probably amazed her.

About a dozen people were in the dining room. No one I knew except Paul and the band. They had just finished a number. As I went by him, I said "Can I talk to you when you're not busy?" I thought it was time to tell him.

He gave me a searching look. "We break after the next number."

I sat down and, at six minutes past nine, I ordered chicken soup and tea. Andrew had apparently been talked into staying with the family till they came home, so I could stop worrying about him. I was glad I had decided to confide in Paul. I wondered if he would think I was brave and noble for having stood up to Mr. Kemel.

The band was going into the last bars of "My Blue Heaven." A new bunch of people came in and sat down behind me. Waiters moved silently around the room. I never saw who dropped the piece of paper onto the table at my left hand. I saw it flutter down and I grabbed it. It said:

Come to appointed place quick.
Andrew

It was Andrew's handwriting.

I saw the surprise and alarm in Paul's face as I ran past the bandstand toward the door. I heard the exclamation of the waiter that I bumped into. Then I was outside in the warm night, running toward the mausoleum as fast as I had ever run in my life.

eleven

MY THOUGHTS raced as fast as my feet, on that endless trip from the hotel to Tamerlane's tomb. They had Andrew, that was clear. It was his handwriting, but they had made him write it. It was not his language. I couldn't imagine old Andy saying "appointed place" unless someone were dictating to him. And, of course, he would have had no way of sending me a message like that by himself, and no reason unless he was in trouble.

Outside the kiosk where we had bought Mother's

cloth, I crashed into a couple of teen-aged boys and nearly knocked one of them down. I saw the crash coming, but I was going too fast to avoid it. I spun off into the street and then kept on going without slowing down. I didn't even have enough breath to say *sorry*. I heard them yell after me—Russian cussing, I suppose. People sitting out in the warm evening in front of their adobe houses turned to look at me, probably in amazement, as I raced by them. Once I turned my ankle, when I jumped the dry ditch between the sidewalk and the street. It hurt, but I kept on going, limping.

Limping. That rotten Kemel. If he had hurt my brother, I was going to kill him with my bare hands. They must have snatched Andrew as he was coming home from the campus. I was glad now that I'd told him about the encounter with Kemel; at least he'd know what it was all about, if that was any comfort. I wondered if they'd grabbed Andrew after nine o'clock, when they knew I wasn't coming, or before. Mr. Kemel must have been pretty sure I wouldn't come.

I turned into the wide courtyard and slowed down. I didn't want to advertise my arrival. For the first time, I began to wonder what I was going to do. Of course they were expecting me, waiting for me. I crouched in the shadow of the wall, trying to calm down my breathing. I couldn't see or hear anything.

I began to move slowly toward the entrance to the tombs, keeping close to the wall. It seemed to me everybody in Samarkand could hear me breathing. My rib cage was going up and down like a yo-yo. I felt as if I were being watched by a thousand pairs of eyes. It was a very creepy feeling. Up till then I'd been too upset to think about what might happen to Andrew and me, but now all the possibilities began to crowd my mind. There were the two of us now who knew that Mr. Kemel had an illegal package for Moscow. How would he react to that? Would he try to frame us with whatever it was? If the police found us with either smuggled jewels or dope . . . Or what if he got violent? What if he and that head creep of his had already harmed Andrew? . . .

I gave up any attempt at taking them by surprise. I ran into the big dark room where the caskets were. I could see the dim, rectangular outlines, but for a minute I couldn't see anything else.

Then there was a muffled sound and a scraping just beyond the dark jade coffin of Tamerlane. I started around the end of it and a tall figure rose up right in front of me. Kemel, of course. And at his side on the floor lay Andrew, gagged and trussed up like a Christmas turkey. The man in the black skullcap was bending over him.

At least for a couple of seconds I took them by surprise. I gave Mr. Kemel a very sharp elbow in the stomach, and I threw myself at the other guy, getting him around the knees. He gave a little yell and he fell backward and cracked his head on one of the other coffins. He didn't move, and I thought I had killed him. Meanwhile, Andy was thrashing around on the floor trying to get loose.

I bent down to help him, but Mr. Kemel, who was still clutching his stomach, grabbed me by the hair with his other hand and hauled me up.

"My dear Miss Harlow," he said, "I just wished to speak with you. There was no need for all this violence."

"Then why is my brother tied up?"

"I thought you might need a bit of persuasion." Still holding my hair, he leaned down and took the gag out of Andrew's mouth. Andrew spat.

"Are you all right?" I asked.

"I guess so." He tried to get up, but he couldn't.

"Untie him," I said. I don't know what gave me the idea I could give the orders.

"First, we must transact our business," Kemel said. The man on the floor groaned. Kemel gave him a little kick. "Get up," he said in English, and then a long speech in what I guess was Turkish. The man got up, holding his head. I thought it was just as well he wasn't dead. Then he gave me a murderous look, and I changed my mind.

"Let go of my hair," I said to Kemel.

"Very well, but please try not to be so impetuous." He let go. He pulled a package out of a canvas knapsack that lay on the floor. The package was wrapped in thick paper with lots of string, and it was sealed in several places with sealing wax. When you send a package in Russia, they seal it like that after they've inspected it, but I suppose he had done this himself. "This is the package for my daughter." He gave me a long look.

"I don't want to take it."

"No, I realize that. But you will not be sorry. And you see," he said, with what I guess you could call a sinister little smile, "you have no choice. I dislike forcing you to do something against your will, Miss Harlow, believe me I do, but the matter is of such importance that I, too, in a sense have no choice."

"Don't take it," Andrew said. He ducked as the other guy started to kick him.

Kemel stopped him with another flood of Turkish. "You see," Kemel said to me, "we are not playing games here. You are children, but you are in grown-up situations now, as fate would have it. You will listen carefully." He spoke slowly. "You will place this package inside the boy's blue cloth bag."

Andrew said, "How do you know I have a . . ." But he stopped when the skullcap man raised his arm.

"Listen carefully." Kemel's voice was sharper. "Time is short. Tomorrow you will fly as planned to Moscow, where you will change planes for New York. When you come off the plane in Moscow, you will as usual be met by an Intourist guide, who will occupy himself or herself with your parents. You will lag slightly behind. As you approach the terminal building, a woman will come toward you—brown hair, red coat—she is about forty years old. She will nod to you and smile. You will make sure that you are not observed. You will slip package out of boy's bag and hand it to her. She will disappear at once. That is all." He smiled broadly. "You see how simple."

"What if I won't do it?"

"That would be a sad mistake."

"What if I took it and gave it to the police?"

He gave me a pitying smile. "How foolish. An American in possession of smuggled goods . . . The KGB would be most interested."

"I would tell them about Mr. Kemel."

He laughed. "There is no Mr. Kemel." He said something to his sidekick, and the man pulled out a wicked-looking long knife and leaned toward Andrew. I yelled. Mr. Kemel grabbed my arm hard. "Do not do that. He is untying your brother."

The man sliced the rope, and Andrew got up, stiff and unsteady.

"You see, I keep my word," Kemel said. "I release him. But you see how easy it was to get him. I have people in Moscow who are just as competent, believe me. It would be most dangerous to do anything reckless." He held out the package to me. "You remember your instructions?"

"Yes." I looked at that shiny knife that the man held in his right hand. It was unpleasantly close to Andrew's neck. I reached for the package.

Suddenly we were blinded by a bright light, and somebody was yelling in Russian. Kemel ducked and tried to slide out of the circle of light. The man with the knife grabbed for Andrew, but as he seized Andrew's shirt collar somebody hurtled past me and grabbed the man. Then everything happened at once. It was Paul, who was struggling on the floor

with the man with the knife, and two Soviet police-
men had grabbed Kemel. A third policeman went to
help Paul. They got the knife, and the policeman
dragged the man forward to where Kemel was. Paul,
who was disheveled and bleeding from a cut on the
cheek, reached out and grabbed both Andy and me
by the hands and pulled us close to him. There was
an awful lot of talking going on in Russian. I was
distressed to find that I was crying.

We were bundled into one police car, Kemel and his man into another. At the police station, Andrew and I were questioned at length, and all we said was taped. The police were very nice to us, and the one who had helped Paul said we were brave children.

They didn't tell us anything about Kemel, and when Andrew asked, they pretended not to understand. A policewoman made a summary on paper of what we had said on tape and we signed it. I was worried about Paul, and I made a big point of what a good friend he had been to us. I did not say that he had been approached by Kemel because I was afraid it would get him into trouble. Andrew didn't mention it either. I kept remembering how Paul had not wanted to get involved with the police at all, and how he had done it for us.

It was a great relief to find him waiting for us when we came out. He looked all right. Somebody had given him a strip of plaster for the cut on his face. A police driver took us back to the hotel.

Nobody was in the lobby but us. We sat down on the sofa near the elevator. Andrew was shaking like a leaf.

"It was my fault, Sis," he said. "I talked the family into letting me leave. I went by the mausoleum to see if anybody was hanging around." He made a face. "They were."

"Stop worrying, duck. It's all over." I got out my

comb and combed his hair. "Why don't you go take a hot shower and go to bed."

"What if our parents are back? Shall I tell them?"

"We'll worry about that later. They're probably not in yet." It was hard to believe it wasn't yet 10:30. "I'll be up in a minute."

Andrew got up and looked at Paul. "Thanks for saving us. I'm sorry I thought you might be a junkie."

Paul smiled. "It's better to wonder about such things than to think all is goodness and innocence. Are you all right, Andrew? You feel all right?"

"Sure." The color began to come back into his cheeks. He started to turn away and then he stopped. "What was in the box?"

"A necklace."

I gasped. Was it true, then, about Grandpa and his little girl?

But then Paul said, "That was on top. The box had a hollow bottom. Full of hashish."

"Was it a very valuable necklace?" I said.

"I don't think so. Those stones, you know, that they sell in the shops . . ."

"Semiprecious."

Andrew nodded. "I'd hate to have got roughed up for nothing. So long, Paul. See you before we go?"

Paul said yes, and Andrew went upstairs. It felt nice to know that no menace was lurking around spying on us.

I said, "I guess we've led awfully sheltered lives. I mean it's hard to believe it all happened to us."

"Unfortunately such things do happen. In your country as well."

"Yes. You think of it as just on TV."

"Did you also think I was in the drug business?"

"No. You wouldn't do something like that."

Paul looked sad. "A man does things he isn't proud of." Then he smiled at me. "But no, not that."

"Do you love Penny?" I hadn't known I was going to say it, but it seemed like a good night for truth.

He didn't answer at once. "Penny is a beautiful girl. It is easy to be a little in love with her. But she will have many men in love with her. One would face much competition." He smiled. "I do not like competition."

"Well, you're safe with me. The line that is supposed to form on the right has never showed up."

He looked puzzled.

"I mean, I'm not what you'd call in great demand."

"Give yourself time. You are just beginning to grow up."

"Many nights like tonight and I'll be old before my time." I took a deep breath. "I suppose you know I'm in love with you." I could feel myself turning red.

He touched my wrist very lightly. "I am honored."

I felt as if I had to talk, I don't know why. I told him all kinds of things, about my track record, my friends at school, my math teacher that I had a crush on last year, my weight problem, the new diet-and-exercise routine and the necklace I was going to reward myself with. I talked so much, I was appalled, but he listened very sympathetically.

When I finally ran down, he said, "You will make the goal. You will always make the goal, like your races in the hundred yards. You are a girl of will and determination, and much goodness. I hope you will always be my friend."

He wrote down my address, but he wouldn't give me his because he said he was always roaming around. At last, he walked me to the elevator. "Sleep well. You have a long trip tomorrow."

"Will I see you again?" I could hardly bear to leave him. I was more than in love with him now; he was my own dear friend.

"I will see you go." He stood there until the elevator door closed between us.

Penny came in before I went to sleep. She, Pyotr, Ivan and Masha had been to a wedding, and had a wonderful time. She told me all about it. In fact, she was so friendly, I told her I was sorry I had messed up her makeup.

"That's all right," she said. "I'll get you some of

your own for your birthday."

Which reminded me of Andrew's birthday. I thought I might put up the down payment on a microscope if Dad would do the rest.

"What did you and Andy do on your last night in Samarkand?" Penny asked, as she got into bed.

"Oh, we went over to Tamerlane's tomb and played cops and robbers."

She yawned and put out the light. "When are you going to grow up?"

twelve

E DECIDED to put off telling the family till we got home. When there was half a world between us and what had happened, maybe it wouldn't shock them so much. No one knew about it but Paul, and of course the police, but the Soviets don't spread that kind of thing around as news. So in all the hustle and bustle of travel we just let it go, though my mother wondered how Andrew's shirt got so dirty.

Paul saw us off, carrying our bags to the Intourist car at the hotel and packing them in himself. He gave my mother and Penny each a pretty corsage and he gave Andrew a pair of his drumsticks. His gift to me was a small package, and he said so only Andrew and I could hear, "Don't worry, it's not what you think," and we all laughed like people with a special secret.

I opened it on the plane, when Andrew had his nose to the window studying the Aeroflot jet. It was a piece of beautiful Russian amber. He had enclosed a note, in neat angular handwriting.

For my dear friend Hardy, for her necklace, which will be long and beautiful as I wish her life to be also.

> Devotedly,
> *Paul*

When the family saw the amber, Penny was visibly impressed. "What does he mean about a necklace? He didn't give me a present."

"He gave you those sweet flowers," my mother said.

I had to tell them about the necklace. I couldn't think of any way out. They were nice, even Penny. She said, "I'll pay your way to Weight Watchers if you want to go."

"I suppose," my father said, "Andrew will require a drum to go with those drumsticks."

"No," Andrew said, "I'm going to dry some hide and make my own."

No one asked him where he'd get the hide. When boys are Andrew's age, there are questions better not asked.

When we got to the Moscow airport, I was scared stiff. I hung on to Andrew the whole time and I stayed so close to my father, he finally said, "Hardy, I do value your close attention but you are tripping me up."

I never saw a forty-year-old woman in a red coat. I suppose the grapevine must have been working. I wondered if there really was a little girl somewhere who would have gotten the necklace of semiprecious stones. If so, I wished her good luck.

I didn't relax until we were on the plane for Kennedy. I was sitting in front of my parents and I was half-asleep when I heard my father say, "I wonder if we'll ever hear from Popov."

"I rather thought he'd come to see us off," my mother said.

"No, he'd done his bit." There was silence for a minute. "He was KGB, you know."

I heard the astonishment in my mother's voice, and I must say I felt astonishment, too. "Secret police?" She kept her voice low.

"Oh, yes. I thought so from the start. All those questions."

"But, Harold, was he watching *you?*"

"Sure." My father sounded amused. "Not everyone finds me the figure of righteousness that you do."

"But an academic man!"

"What better place? Oh, they're all over. They have to be, I suppose, given the assumption that that huge and varied collection of peoples is to be run in a certain way. It could easily get out of hand."

"I thought Professor Popov was a friend."

"He was, in his own way. He treated us royally."

"I'll never trust anyone again."

My father chuckled. "Yes, you will. Tomorrow. You're a natural-born truster."

I stared out the window at the clouds. At that moment I felt older and more experienced than my mother. I wished I could tell her what I had found out: that you don't have to choose between either trusting everybody or trusting nobody. You just have to learn to use your head, observe, think. Not go off half-cocked. Not be oversuspicious like the KGB or naive like my mother. I wondered how my father had caught on about Professor Popov. But I guess if you knew it might happen, you'd sense it when it did. I thought about Professor Popov and Mr. Kemel. He must have been checking him out, too. Well, if he was, he missed the boat. Mr. Kemel was apprehended by that internationally renowned detective team, Harlow and Harlow. Not really, I guess, but it would make a dandy theme.

When I told Andrew later about Popov, he said, "Then he must have known all about our last night in Samarkand. I mean he would, wouldn't he?"

We kept putting off telling the family. Somehow it was hard to bring it up. And with the excitement of getting back to school and all, we were too busy for fireside chats. But one evening, Dad came into the dining room carrying his Dubonnet in one hand and a letter in the other. Behind his back, Andrew mouthed, "Popov," and clutched his head. I felt panicky. It wouldn't do at all to have them hear about our adventure from the professor.

"Dad," I said, "we have something to tell you . . ."

Dad was slitting open the envelope. "Just a minute. Got a letter from Popov."

"Can I have the stamp?" Even in emergencies Andrew is practical.

My father read the letter, frowned, read it again. "Sometimes I think my grasp of the Russian language is slipping." He looked up. "When did this letter come, incidentally? I didn't see it when I got home."

"I hid it," Andrew said.

"Hid it? Hid my mail?"

"I wondered how it got behind the gravy bowl,"

my mother said. "Andrew dear, whatever for?"

"May one ask why you hid my mail?" To my father mail is sacred. It would almost be safer to hide his wife and children.

"Because Hardy wasn't here," Andrew said.

"Because Hardy wasn't here." My father looked at Andrew as if he had suddenly flipped.

"It's because we have to tell you something," I said. "First."

Penny said impatiently, "But what does Professor Popov say? Does he mention Ivan and Pyotr?"

My father shook out the pages that were covered with Cyrillic script. "He says, in his florid Russian manner, that he enjoyed our visit, that he hopes I

have forgiven him for a certain degree of scrupulosity (which is the only translation I can think of) in his attitude, which came from on high . . ." He threw a significant look at my mother. "That he wishes to express his admiration for the fortitude and daring of our children, which has come to his attention, and to assure me that the great Soviet people will forever be indebted to them . . ." He frowned and looked up. "To *my* children? . . . 'as they make their way toward the gleaming light of socialist truth.' " He looked at us. "You didn't join the Party, did you?"

"Dad," I said, "you'd really better listen. Why don't you carve the lamb while I explain."

It took my father a long time to carve that roast. At first they thought Andy and I were making it all up. Then they asked a million questions and my mother gave a thousand small shrieks of dismay and alarm. Then we got the lecture on trying to handle things that were beyond us, and the difference between independence and bone-headed obstinacy.

"How," my father said at last, "could a man as eminently rational as I am produce such a pair of wild-eyed James Bonds?"

"Don't look at me," my mother said. "There's never been anything of that sort on my side of the family."

Unexpectedly Penny said, "I think that they were

kind of brave."

"The Byzantine quality of the whole affair boggles the mind," said my father.

And my mother said, "Who would have thought, that pleasant Mr. Kemel."

Later my father read us part of his letter to Professor Popov. He wrote:

Thank you for your kind words about our two youngest. If they were able to thwart to any degree the wickedness of your enemies, we are pleased. We have tried to bring them up to be resourceful, independent and honorable.

That night as Andrew had his eye glued to his new microscope, examining a *volvox,* he said, "It's crazy, isn't it. I mean we really didn't do anything. We just fell into all that. Grownups are too much."

I didn't argue the point, but we really had *done things*. Things that got us involved. I'd fallen for Paul. We'd been curious. I'd listened to Mr. Kemel. Andrew had walked by the mausoleum and right into Kemel's hands. I had gone after him. And so on. And although all our lives we'd said to each other, "Grownups are too much," or "Grownups can't be depended on," and all that, I was getting awfully close to being a grownup myself, and it wouldn't be so long for old Andy either. The wall between kids and grownups dissolves fast, once it starts to go. Which I found kind of an exciting idea, though I knew it would be repulsive to Andrew.

Paul sends me a postcard now and then from different places in Eastern Europe. He always asks how the necklace is coming. Actually I'll probably have it done in about three months. With luck.

Pages from the travel book of Mary Harding (Hardy) Harlow:

Notes on Tamerlane: Name also spelled Tamburlaine, corrupted from Timur-i-lenk, meaning Lame Timar. Lived 1335–1405. Born at Kesh, now Shakhrisyabz. His dad supposedly head of a tribe, and an ancestor was allegedly related to Genghis Khan. (Note: Brittanica and Intourist don't agree. If I write paper for Miss Anderson, use Brittanica facts. If for Miss Rhodes, use Intourist, and label the source. She can then give her lecture on propaganda, its faults and foibles.)

Tamerlane began rabble-rousing at an early age.

Right in there whenever there was a disturbance. Some guy invaded Samarkand in 1361 and made Tamerlane his minister. T. shortly split the scene and wandered around with brother-in-law, wreaking havoc. (See Gibbon's *Decline and Fall of Roman Empire*.)

Got his brother-in-law assassinated, proclaimed himself head of the Chagatai Khans and the Mongol empire. Returned to Samarkand.

Next ten years fought Turkestan and assorted others, helped the Khan of the Crimea fight Russia. Occupied Moscow, beat Lithuanians.

1383 Conquest of Persia. Took over also Armenia, Iraq, Mesopotamia, Georgia (the dirty dog!). Was beaten by the Golden Horde (yea!) Then chased Golden Horde into Russian Steppes. (Sob!) Tamerlane massacred whole cities and built towers of his victims' skulls (recycling, fourteenth century-style).

1398 Invaded India. (The man must have had strong arches. All those distances!) He was now past sixty. Ruined Delhi. Used ninety elephants to bring stones from India to Samarkand to build his mosque.

Set out for Egypt. Conquered Azerbaijan, marched on Syria, sacked Aleppo, occupied Damascus.

1401 Took Baghdad, slew 20,000. Wintered in Georgia (needed a short breather, no doubt). Invaded Anatolia, captured Smyrna.

1404 Back at the ranch in Samarkand. Set out in

December to conquer China. Got sick in January and died. Embalmed in an *ebony* coffin. (Brittanica says "ebony," not jade). Shipped back to Samarkand. *Sic gloria transit.*

He was very tall, had a big head and a red face, and his hair was white from childhood. One could safely conclude that he created a stir in his lifetime.

—M.H.H.

Notes from the journal of Andrew W. Harlow:

SAMARKAND, city of:

Geography: altitude 2330! Located in valley of Zeravshain River. 168 miles from Tashkent, north of Afghanistan.

Weather: Sunny, generally cloudless. No frost for 200 days of year. Warm breezes from desert.

Resources: marble, granite, gypsum. Agricultural products: e.g., cotton, fruit, sheep (Karakul type), goats.

Short history of: Fourth century B.C. known as
  Maracanda[1.]

Captured by Alexander the Great, 329.

Became part of Turkish Khaqanate, sixth century A.D.

Captured by Arabs, eighth century.

Ruled by Samanids[2.] Ninth and tenth century.

Captured by the Kara Kitais[3.] Twelfth century.

Captured by Khorezm[4.] Thirteenth century.

Captured by Genghis Khan 1220.

Revolted against Mongols 1365.

Capitol of Timur's[5.] empire, end of fourteenth
  century.

Under Timur became most important economic
  and cultural center of Central Asia. Situated
  on trade routes, e.g., the Silk Road from
  China.

Conquered by Uzbeks 1550.

Ruled by Shaibanids[6.] who moved away[7.]

Attacked by nomads and Persians seventeenth
  and eighteenth centuries.

1720–1770: totally uninhabited!

1868– Russians took over and made it capital
  of Samarkand province.

1924– Soviets made it capital of Uzbek Soviet
  Socialist Republic.

1930– Lost position as capital to Tashkent.

Miscellaneous: The "Old Town" dates from Middle Ages. "New Town" dates from Russian conquest 1868.

Streets converge toward center from original six gates in eleventh century wall (Now destroyed).

Present city has university,[8.] colleges of agriculture and medicine.

Irrigation required.

Footnotes
(1.) Capital of Sogdiana.
(2.) Note to myself: Who were Samanids?
(3.) Note to myself: Who were Kara Kitais?
(4.) Note to myself: Who were Khorezm?
(5.) Tamerlane.
(6.) Note to myself: Who were Shaibanids?
(7.) Why?
(8.) Founded 1933.